Coveted by the Bear

By T. S. Joyce

Coveted by the Bear
ISBN-13: 978-1505871692
ISBN-10: 1505871697
Copyright © 2015, T. S. Joyce
First electronic publication: January 2015

T. S. Joyce
www.tsjoycewrites.wordpress.com

All Rights Are Reserved. No part of this book may be used or reproduced in any manner whatsoever without written permission, except in the case of brief quotations embodied in critical articles and reviews. The unauthorized reproduction or distribution of this copyrighted work is illegal. No part of this book may be scanned, uploaded or distributed via the Internet or any other means, electronic or print, without the author's permission.

NOTE FROM THE AUTHOR:
This book is a work of fiction. The names, characters, places, and incidents are products of the writer's imagination or have been used fictitiously and are not to be construed as real. Any resemblance to persons, living or dead, actual events, locale or organizations is entirely coincidental. The author does not have any control over and does not assume any responsibility for third-party websites or their content.

Published in the United States of America

First digital publication: January 2015
First print publication: January 2015

For Corinne.
Where would I be without you?
(Hint: Swimming in a sea of misplaced commas.)

Other Books by T. S. Joyce

Wolf Brides
Wolf Bride
Red Snow Bride
Dawson Bride

Bear Valley Shifters
The Witness and the Bear
Devoted to the Bear
Return to the Bear
Betray the Bear
Redeem the Bear

Hells Canyon Shifters
Call of the Bear
Fealty of the Bear
Avenge the Bear
Claim the Bear
Heart of the Bear

Chapter One
Caleb

The bell dinged above the front door of Jake's Quickstop. My brothers and I turned our heads from our conversation just enough to see who had come in. It was a small town. Everyone knew everyone.

Old man Tucker sauntered in and called out a greeting to Bernard behind the counter. I nodded my hello when he waved in our direction.

"Here you go, boys," the waitress said, setting three full plates down in front of Evan, Brian, and me.

She wore a red and white, tight-fitting dress with white sneakers. The dress looked young for her, but she had been working at Jake's for as long as I could remember. The uniform had never changed. She'd probably filled it out nicely in her twenties.

"Thanks, Leona," I said through a smile before I dug in. I was starving. Working on an oil rig meant physical effort and exertion from the moment I stepped onto that platform until the moment I climbed back down the clanking metal stairs to my truck. I was always hungry enough to eat a horse when my shift ended.

Jake's was quite the hotspot in town. It had multiple functions for a rancher or an oilman on the go. It tripled as a grocery store, gas station, and fine dining. By fine dining, I meant the best burgers and fried burritos in town. It was also Bryson's social apex where all the old ladies picked up on the latest gossip. A boisterous group of them chattered away at the booth nearest the casino machine and rack of Twizzlers.

The bell above the door dinged again, but I didn't look up. The burger was good enough to hold my attention. Jake's grew eerily quiet. The kind of quiet you feel more than you hear. Even the old ladies had stopped their chattering. Evan elbowed me, but I was already turning my head to see who had caused friction in a room full of old friends.

"It's Crazy Mira," Evan whispered.

I could hear the smile in his words. When Crazy Mira came to town, everyone had enough entertainment to last them a week.

Each member of the crowd had frozen in whatever position they had been in when she came through the door. The audience held more interest for me than Crazy Mira did. Nelda Jenkins had a string of pasta hanging out of her mouth like she had been mid-slurp when the girl had arrived. It dangled there.

Nelda reminded me of a fishing trip I had taken with my dad. The water had been so uncharacteristically clear, we could see the green and brown backs of the fish we were after. I had plunked my worm in the water in front of a big one and waited, a trill sounding through me as the fish moved closer. I had never seen anything like it, but the fish clamped on and stayed there. I didn't even feel the pull of the pole. We just stayed tethered to each other by this thin, almost invisible line while he started to digest my worm. I had often wondered if I would ever feel so tethered to another living creature again.

Nelda's worm didn't know it was being eaten yet.

I could hear the sharp intake of air from Mira when she looked up enough to notice Jake's was abnormally busy for this time of day. The girl was swimming in a cloud of mystery, but that she tried to avoid people wasn't one of them. She'd failed.

Mira dropped her chin to her chest and skittered for the grocery aisles. She picked up a small blue plastic basket from an end cap and began to fill it with items from a list she held clenched tightly in her white-knuckled grip.

I tried to ignore her, if for nothing else than to give her peace from one pair of prying eyes. My gaze kept drifting just far enough in her direction to catch her movement in my peripheral, though. Something about the strange woman demanded attention.

I saw Nelda make the sign for the devil with her hands. If ever anyone mentioned a witch, people knew who they were talking about. Crazy Mira and witch were one in the same.

Nelda's gesture at Mira pissed me off, but for the life of me, I couldn't figure out why.

"Did you hear about Dina Manchester?" I asked Evan, loud enough for the others to hear.

Evan still looked dumbly in Mira's direction.

It was my other brother, Brian, who took the bait. "No. Why, did you hear something?"

"Nope. Just wondering why she put off the wedding. Again."

The ladies in the booth looked at each other with wide eyes and started to whisper amongst themselves.

Crazy Mira's movements became less jerky and robotic with some of the attention directed elsewhere. She rushed. She didn't get many groceries, but it felt like she'd been in here for hours. Acutely aware of her effect on everything to function normally, I wished she would finish shopping already and leave.

She dropped a can of soup, and the sound of metal on tile cracked through the room. Everyone became quiet and attentive again. She apologized. To the soup? I shook my head. Crazy Mira.

I wasn't hungry anymore so I pushed off and laid a crumpled ten dollar bill on the counter. Leona smiled at me. She probably loved serving the McCreedy boys. We always tipped her what our meal cost. Our dad always taught us that kindness and a good tip kept the spittle out of our food.

"Good burger, as always," I told Leona.

She beamed.

"Why are you leaving so soon?" Evan asked incredulously. What he was really asking was, *why in the hell are you leaving before Crazy Mira finishes her show?*

I shrugged noncommittally. Really, I didn't have an answer. Staring at Crazy Mira had never bothered me before. Now, it left a sick feeling in my stomach.

By the time I turned for the door, Mira had pushed her meager groceries onto the checkout counter. She was staring longingly at a miniature refrigerator filled with small cartons of milk as if they were stacks of Spanish gold.

"Fifteen seventy-six," Bernard told her as he began to bag up the food.

"Oh," she said softly. She counted the change that sat in the bowl of her palm. "I don't have enough." She looked at the goods like she was trying to decide which to put back.

She didn't even ask for Bernard to cut her a break, and something about that struck me. Evan snickered from the counter in the back. Mira apparently heard him, too, because she threw a terrified glance in his direction. The problem was, I was in the midst of leaving and right in her line of sight. She froze when she saw me approaching. I didn't mean to scare her. I was only headed for the door to hear the dinging of the bell that meant salvation from this uncomfortable situation.

I'd never actually looked at her face before. She did an impressive job hiding it with all of that thick, wavy, devil-black hair that cascaded down her back and brushed her hips. She always leaned forward a little, though whether it was to help gravity to pull her hair in front of her face or to look at the ground where she was walking, I couldn't guess. Maybe both. And here she was, terrified. I was the cobra and she was the mouse. Not one of the black and white, hand-reared mice they sold at the feed store, but a gray, matted, feral mouse with teeth. She was the assumed victim none-the-less. I hated her for making me feel this way.

Why couldn't she just act normal? Say *hi* to people? Join a conversation? Smile? It was a small town. Everybody knew everything about everybody, but you couldn't get more people willing to help you than in a place like this.

Despite my anger, I pulled a five dollar bill out of my pocket. "Here," I said as I laid it on the counter with her one dollar bills and coin change.

"No, thank you." Her voice cracked on the last word like she hadn't used it in a while. Mira cleared her throat and looked down. She pushed the five dollar bill back in my direction and took a package of frozen broccoli and a loaf of wheat bread out of the bags. "Now do I have enough?" she asked Bernard.

He shook his head. "Still a dollar ten short," he said in a regretful tone.

"Just take the money," I said a little too loudly. I was baffled. Why was I still standing here trying to help her? And why couldn't she just take the stupid money and give us both an escape?

Mira flinched at the quiet snickering from behind me as if the sound were the crack of thunder in her ear. Her shoulders hunched inward when Evan asked me, "Caleb, what are you doing?"

She threw a determined look at me. "I can't."

I was already angry and should have just left. Instead, I gritted out, "You know, you really are as crazy as everyone says you are."

I regretted the words before they finished leaving my lips. The look on her face was something I would never forget. I watched her drown in sadness, in fear, and humiliation. She wasn't angry with me. She was disappointed in me, and somehow that made it worse. I wasn't usually cruel, and her confusion at my reaction held me in place, unable to take my eyes from her sorrow. The laughter around us had her dark eyes darting from one grinning face to another. She leaned her head forward and stared at the ground for a moment before she scooped up her change and bolted out the front door.

"What about your groceries?" Bernard yelled after her.

The dinging of the bell was the ugliest sound I'd ever heard.

Chapter Two
Mira

Such a fine line was drawn between life and death. No one knew that better than me. I sighed as my stomach ached deeply, and I imagined myself completely hollow.

The low-lying ceiling above my head was dim in the early morning light and covered in plastic stars that still glowed at night despite their age. The room had belonged to my mother before it had been cast into my ownership. I stamped the thought of her down, shoving it behind the locked iron doors in my head. Sometimes, if I did it quickly enough, the pain would be locked away with her memories.

I rubbed my fingers along the puckered scars across my hip bones and wondered what kind of story they would tell to a man who had reason to look at them. I had nothing to worry about. It wasn't as if the boys in town were beating down my door. I smiled privately. God, a fist against my crappy front door would obliterate it. I couldn't hope for even that. People scurried away from me, whispering and shielding their babies, and men felt disinclined to chat with a girl made up entirely of wild hair and disturbing rumors.

In my defense, the hair was a gift from my mother. Damn genetics.

Mother. There it was again. I growled and rolled ungracefully off the side of the bed. My feet and hands hit the floor. Might as well dig around for some clean clothes while I was down here. The search lasted seconds. My uncle, and barely willing guardian, had decided clothes were a thing of necessity only. If he could have gotten away with letting me run around dressed like Mowgli from *The Jungle Book*, he would have set the precedence years ago. That idea had failed when I grew boobs.

Other than the three tossed shirts and the cutoff pair of jean shorts, my room was tidy. I had a tendency to keep the entire house neat. It was as if the chaos of my youth had driven me to organization in adulthood. Okay, so maybe twenty wasn't adulthood to others, but I had grown up long ago. Honestly, I couldn't remember ever being a child.

The first of the morning birds sang its song outside my window, and it made me miss the rooster. He had been delicious. The panes of window glass were streaked and warped with age, and the wood around them held the remnants of what was probably a lovely shade of light blue at some time in the room's history. The walls were bare other than a few pictures I had ripped out of an overdue library book one night when I was feeling especially volatile. They were pinned side-by-side, two pictures of little huts propped above the ocean water with transparent floors to view the fish, squid, crabs, sea stars, and other stuff I couldn't begin to venture a guess at because I'd never actually been to the ocean. I'd never been much of anywhere—an unfortunate by-product of my secrets.

Next to the ripped pages was a small map with a red thumb tack I had not-so-artfully stabbed between the words Bora Bora. *Paradise. My escape.* It was where my mind lent itself when things got so dark I couldn't breathe for fear of dying.

The rest of my walls were just that. Walls. No paint, no decoration, and absolutely no personality to say it was Mira Fletcher's room. Just wooden plank after splintered wooden plank that told the square of my room to stay where it was. The shabby floors here had as much chance of escape as I did.

I had asked Uncle Brady to fix up the room for me when I first moved in. He'd said, "Ain't gonna happen, darlin'. Stuff's more valuable if it's original."

I flared my nostrils at the heady scent of mold and wood rot and thoroughly disagreed.

With seeking hands, I found my cleanest looking shirt, then stood in one fluid motion.

I looked critically into the weathered, rust-eaten mirror over the dresser. Hips, legs, stomach, neck. All looked normal in the marred mirror. In a cleaner one, the scars of my struggles would have stood out like stars against the blackest backdrop of night, shining and dimming in the various stages of age and healing.

Elbows locked, I leaned forward onto the dresser. It buckled and complained under my weight. I glared at my reflection. "I'm gonna kill you…squirrel."

I liked to call what I would hunt. It was my ritual. A weird one, admittedly, but it wasn't as if anyone were watching. No one was ever watching. If ever there was a benefit to being utterly and uncompromisingly alone, shamelessly talking to one's self would be it. And if I happened to be in town when I talked to myself, all the better. Townies would say, "There goes Crazy Mira. That kooky girl has gone to talking to herself now, too."

People asked less of crazy people.

I pulled the threadbare cotton shirt over my head and shimmied into my cut-offs. At a loss for socks, I pulled my boots over bare feet. I'd pay for it later, but there was nothing to be done about that now.

A gurgling growl ripped through me, and I lifted the hem of my shirt out of habit. Brushing my fingertips against the scars over my hip bones again, I weighed my options. Go to town and face the mortifying possibility that Caleb McCreedy might be there to torment me again, or hunt something down. What I couldn't do was sit around and wait for someone to save me. I had to save myself in this life.

I scribbled a quick explanation about where I was going on a sticky note, stuck it to the quiet refrigerator, and then turned to leave. On second thought, the note was unnecessary. The habit had only been for appearances. No one would ever read it or wonder at my whereabouts. It was for show in case some nosy cop came to the doorstep wondering where my guardian was. It had made it easier to convince them he was out to the liquor store in town if there was evidence we still had some sort of communication.

Unless I sprouted the ability to raise the dead, communication with my uncle was definitely off the table.

Turning, I fixated on that note. I had counted down the days, and it had finally arrived. The day I didn't have to fear someone discovering Uncle Brady's untimely death and dragging me by my wild hair to some state home to live out the rest of my adolescence. Today was my twentieth birthday, two years past when I had to worry about the foster care system anymore. *Happy birthday to me.*

It felt strange to celebrate another one alone. It was as if the life I wanted and the life I was living warred with each other in my mind. A million tiny battles fought throughout the day that determined whether I'd stay in the here and now, or if my mind would flit to the relief of daydream. To Bora Bora where my lavish friends and family would bake me cakes and buy me extravagant presents. I didn't actually want or need these things, but the imaginings felt necessary for my continued existence. Knowing there was more to life for others kept me going.

The note plunked satisfyingly into the metal trashcan, and I slid my hand comfortably into the worn leather strap that hooked to the smallest of Uncle Brady's guns. Hefting it over my shoulder, I glanced once more at the house before I left to hunt down something that could ease the ache in my stomach. There was no point in locking the front door. Anyone could kick it in if they were so inclined, and the alarm system of the house was the fact that no one would willingly enter what looked like a meth lab. Unless it was a meth addict looking for meth, in which case, he could have the damned house.

Sure, I'd have to alert the tiny town of Bryson about Uncle Brady's death, and the power in the town wouldn't like it when I enlightened them that my guardian had passed last year. No one had even bothered to wonder why he just stopped showing up to work. Being the town alcoholic enlisted you with some pretty special benefits, such as absolutely no accountability.

I hopped over the missing stair on the front porch and landed with a little dust explosion onto the front lawn. Bull nettle and sticker burrs made up the floral bits of the yard. Yep, I'd have to tell the town about my uncle's passing, and the will he'd left in my care, too, but I didn't have to do any of that right now.

The ground was rough and hard to navigate, even for someone skilled at walking these trails. The potholes and hidden dips created the perpetual danger of a twisted ankle that kept my eyes on the road, but my other senses in the woods. A broken ankle meant no hunting. There would be no bandages and painkillers and time on the couch for me. A broken ankle meant a likely and painful death by starvation.

A sound caught and held my attention. I froze, one leg locked into place and one bent and resting on the toe.

There it was again. The softest of sighs, the barest of whispers. A noise as quiet as a breath. It was the death chant of something that had already accepted its impending doom.

I changed direction. Footstep after quiet footstep steered me toward the noise. I wouldn't have cared if I wasn't so hungry and that sound didn't present the possibility of an easy meal. It's not like I had the ammunition to waste to put the poor creature out of its misery, anyhow.

Or perhaps it was curiosity, pity, or something more that led me closer to the noise.

The leather strap of my weapon zinged against my shoulder as I pulled it off. The click of the safety sounded loud in the quiet of the woods. All had gone still and the hairs began to prickle and raise on my neck.

I bit my bottom lip. A wise woman would just leave. Instinct was a powerful deterrent, and mine was screaming for me to get out of here. My deep hunger, however, failed to get the message and pressed me closer still.

A break in the foliage of my woods revealed something so unexpected and surprising, I stopped and stared at the crumpled thing, dumbfounded. Lifting the rifle, I trained the scope on it out of a sense of self-preservation, though it was likely already dead. I sidestepped, taking a wide and cautious loop around it for a better look.

It was a man. His young face was made to look older by the grit and blood that painted it. As soon as I saw the blond, shoulder-length hair caressing the side of his face, I recognized him.

"Shit," I muttered as I glared at Caleb McCreedy. Gold stubble graced his jaw, and the sunlight reflected off the sharp angles of his face. He was the most alluring man I'd ever seen, but all the looks in the world didn't mean a thing if his heart was black. His hand rested on his chest, like he'd been trying to keep pressure on a wound there when he'd been conscious. Two of his fingers flicked in the barest gesture, like he was hailing someone in his dreams.

He wasn't dead then. Not yet.

I lifted the rifle to see how it felt to train it on someone so cruel. His face was slack in my scope, his fingers still. Perhaps I'd imagined the life I'd seen there.

A bigger movement near a towering oak tree startled me, and as dread slammed into me at the danger I'd really stumbled across, I lifted the gun and pulled the trigger.

The sound was deafening.

Chapter Three
Mira

If I wasn't fairly certain that bear wasn't my neighbor, Eli Emmerson, I would've been happy to eat that giant grizzly. Bear probably tasted like raccoon, greasy and full of sinew, but about now, I'd try anything. I wasn't a people-eater, though, and even if old Eli looked like a feral grizzly laying in the dirt over there, he'd definitely been human once.

I waited, but the body didn't change back to its human form. Maybe when bear men died, they just stayed like that, all furry and powerful looking. The human Eli had been a sickly old man, frail and not long for the grave, but besides his ribs protruding, his bear form looked healthy.

I debated telling the game warden I'd shot the bear, but they weren't native to Texas, and there would be way more questions about why he was on my land than I was prepared to answer. I'd definitely have to leave out the part about him being a bear shifter bent on murdering Bryson's favorite golden boy. Uncle Brady had crowed shifter stories to the game warden before and been rewarded with a twenty-four hour stint in the drunk tank at the police station.

I cast Caleb an angry glare for trespassing and causing me this trouble. Had the idiot even realized he was being hunted?

I walked cautiously over to the giant grizzly with my rifle trained. It wasn't a high caliber. I had been squirrel hunting after all, but my shot had been true, and I had aimed to kill, not to maim. That had been Mr. Eli's mistake. He played with his food. I did not. I poked the glazed eye with the tip of my rifle to assure myself he was really dead. It didn't flinch.

Kneeling down, I looked with pity at the deceased horse Caleb had apparently ridden onto my land. It had been a beautiful creature. Probably worth ten times the two I had in the rickety old barn out back. Why the hell was Mr. Eli on my land hunting? He'd made a pact with my uncle long ago he'd stay in his own territory, the other side of the fence that separated our properties. I shook my head and frowned. His boys had been killed by poachers a few years back, and he hadn't been the same after that. I'd hardly seen him since he told Uncle Brady what had happened to his family.

Maybe, he finally just lost it.

A soft groan escaped Caleb's parted lips, and I twisted to look back at him. At least the puddle of blood beneath him was probably keeping him cool. See? There was always a bright side to everything.

I squatted down beside him, the tendons of my ankles stretching. I canted my head to the side to get a better look at the wounds around his neck and chest.

"You got yourself messed up bad, didn't you?" I looked back in the direction of the house. It was a long walk from here on an empty stomach, much less dragging a body that weighed twice mine.

I could leave him here.

This wasn't my concern. Caleb was trespassing, anyway. I had rights to shoot him, and I hadn't even done that. I'd gone one step farther and shot his murderer. Avenged his death. I was basically a saint.

I growled in frustration. That wasn't me. No matter what the man had done, I was already moving to try and save him. It wouldn't work, but I had to live with myself. I didn't need another ghost haunting my nightmares. My dance card was full.

I tore Caleb's shirt to admire the damage. It was easy to do because it was already in tatters. Still, I had always wondered what it felt like to rip through fabric so easily. One time when I was younger, I had tried to rip my own shirt open like the hulk. My arms were much too weak, and all I did was growl a lot and stretch the neck so much that my foster parents at the time had grounded me for two weeks. Hulk fans, they were not.

"All right," I said aloud, trying to calm my nerves at touching another human. I couldn't remember the last time my fingers had brushed another's skin. It had been years, at least.

The shirt Caleb wore was useless. Less than useless. It was in shreds and matted with blood in various stages of drying. It was stiff and dirty and smelled of death. When some poor creature lost too much, there was a subtle variation in the smell—an almost unnoticeable shift. That difference in smell meant there was no taking back what had been done, no healing, no more walking this world.

It was close with Caleb.

I tossed the rags to the side and kicked dirt over the top of them. I wasn't going to help the other predators in the area smell the ready-made meal any easier. Right now, Caleb was easy pickings for the hogs that ran rampant here.

I pulled my thin shirt over my head. Self-consciousness didn't cross my mind as I didn't see the man regaining consciousness anytime soon, if ever again. I tried for the second time in my life to hulk rip a shirt with the exact same result—stretched fabric and annoyance.

"Bite the stitches," said a gruff voice as soft as a whisper.

One impossibly blue slit of color looked back at me, appearing even brighter with all of the red surrounding it. Caleb closed his eye and sighed as he slipped into unconsciousness again. I arched my eyebrows at my exposed breasts. For the first time in my life, a boy had seen me basically naked, and the moment had passed so quickly I hadn't even been able to fully appreciate it. Huh. I puffed air out of my mouth. Such a moment should have been huge. At least that's what the books I had read hinted at.

I did as Caleb suggested and got the rip started. With my shirt shredded into exactly two un-strip like pieces, I tied one around a deep gash and puncture wounds at his neck and the other at three deep claw marks across the inside of one of his elbows. They looked the worst. I worked like I was in a trance. I had seen too much blood to be affected by it now. Before I'd come to live with Uncle Brady, my life had been bathed in it.

Caleb should've been dead already. I didn't want to be a pessimist, but this man had lost too much blood to survive. I narrowed my eyes at the still lump of Mr. Eli's body. That rangy old shifter had either ruined Caleb's life or killed him.

The rifle clunked into the inside of Caleb's arm as I set it down. Bolting down the dusty path, I ran like hell for the horses. He could shoot himself or shoot the pigs that would come for him soon. Either way, the choice was his.

I shook like the last leaf on a tree in autumn. The one that was afraid to fall for fear of the unknown. Even when all of his friends had fallen, trembling uncertainty consumed such a leaf before it preformed its final floating dance to meet the fate of the others on the forest floor. It needn't worry, but how could it know it would be reborn the next spring?

I shook for other reasons. Caleb had scared me off buying

groceries, and I hadn't built the nerve to go back yet. It had been a week with nothing in the pantry, and a damning fear of facing Mr. Bernard and the audience at Jake's Quickstop again.

The leaf and I were the same—fearful creatures.

By the time my horse, Bobby, was saddled, I was close to passing out. "Stay awake, stay awake, stay awake," I chanted to the hoof beats of my running stead. Stead was perhaps the wrong word when applied to my twenty-two year old gray gelding that had gone long in the tooth. The uneven terrain kept us at a slower pace than my beating heart preferred, a fact for which Bobby was probably grateful. When I found Caleb again, he was clutching onto the rifle with a shaking hand. It was the only part of him that had moved, and my heart lurched into my throat. I had known that kind of fear before, and I wouldn't have wished it on anyone. Not even Caleb McCreedy.

The saddle creaked as I slid off Bobby. I pulled on his reins, but he balked at the smell of dead predator and blood. The gap between the horse and Caleb's withering body widened. No good.

I tied Bobby off at the nearest tree and ran for the bear. I yanked and pulled on its tail until the body gave a little, then used the momentum to drag him as best as my weakened body could manage. I made it about ten yards before my shaking legs refused another inch. I kicked leaves over the animal to help mask the smell, but it wouldn't do much. I tried Bobby again. He made it close enough to Caleb, but he sure as hell wasn't gracious about it.

"Caleb," I wheezed, finding it increasingly difficult to catch my breath. "Caleb," I tried again as I shook his shoulder gently.

He groaned.

I looked up to the sky. "A little help?" I asked to no answer. It was probable that I'd placed one too many flaming bags of dog turds on God's doorstep to earn any assistance. "Just you and me," I said to Caleb whose eyes rolled back and forth under his closed eyelids.

Hands under his arms and pull.
Rest.
Pull.
Rest.
Pull.
Bobby backed up.
I cursed.
Dragged Bobby closer.
"Caleb!" Teeth gritted against the effort of propping him up. Caleb yelled in pain.
"Help me get you up, and you can pass out on me again," I implored.

Caleb's knees bent and his muscles moved and twitched just enough to get him standing and leaning against Bobby.

Bobby shied.

I cursed again.

Caleb grunted in pain and effort as he hoisted himself upward. He passed out lopsided.

I pushed him onto a sidestepping Bobby.

I clambered on, clenched the saddle horn, and swallowed a sob at how pitiful my body felt.

Squeezing Caleb in place with my knees, I held on tight. "Bobby, home."

I kept staring at the blood stain on Bobby's neck. It was such a stark contrast to his light gray coat. In any other situation, the colors together would have struck me as beautiful. Not today, though. I would never forget this ride for the rest of my life.

When we finally made it back to the house, we slid off the saddle together like we had no bones at all. I lay curled in the dirt beside Caleb's still body. I wretched over and over until my stomach was empty, but my stubborn body tried one more time to the same result. My hands shook so badly, I had trouble using them. Cold sweat dotted my forehead, and the edges of my vision blurred. Maybe Caleb McCreedy and I would die here together in the dirt in front of this old haunted house. The thought of it made the corners of my lips turn up in a pained smile.

He was no Romeo, and I couldn't be further from Juliet if I tried.

I crawled up the stairs and stood unsteadily to let myself in the house. For the hundredth time, I searched the pantry in the kitchen for something to eat. Anything that would keep me up and useful to Caleb. It was empty, as it had been for days. I didn't even try to check the old fridge. The generator had gone out three months after Uncle Brady died, and I hadn't been able to figure out a way to fix it. I suspected the smell of that fridge alone could kill me. The door stayed firmly shut.

I was going to pass out soon, but Caleb couldn't just lay there in direct sunlight. With the last bit of my strength, I dragged him up the stairs and into the front room of my uncle's house. Caleb was probably dead already. I fell hard on my backside and lay down in defeat. I'd fought it longer than I thought I would've been able to.

Caleb lay there, face up in my living room. I tried to see if he was breathing but my attention was pulled in all directions, and it was hard to focus. I closed my eyes and opened them slowly. They grew so heavy, I couldn't keep them open any longer.

At least when I was unconscious, I didn't feel the hunger.

Bright side.

Chapter Four
Caleb

Lips parted, I cleared my throat. The rasp sounded as dry as the south side of a cactus growing in the sand. I was so thirsty, surely I'd die of it. I turned my head to the side and jerked back with pain. "Sss," I hissed, drawing air through my teeth.

I'd known pain. I was a man, and Lord knew I'd done some dumb shit in my day that got me really hurt, but I'd never felt pain like this. I was burning.

Searing flames engulfed every surface of skin I possessed. The wooden ceiling above me offered little to focus on. The wood was an aged dark gray and unpainted. Other than the tattered white curtains that had seen better days over the front window, the house remained untouched. Unadorned. Uncared for.

A low grumbling noise sent my heart into a panic. Adrenaline laced my veins as my brain screamed that the grizzly had followed me here. It was back to finish the job.

Nothing happened.

Another grumble sounded, this one more pathetic than the last. I turned my head gingerly to the side, wincing as clotted injuries stretched and reopened. Crazy Mira lay on her side, completely unconscious. Was she dying? At some point in the throes of pain, she had lifted her knees to her chest and wrapped her thin arms around her abdomen. The position shielded most of her frame from me. I looked at her face. It was relaxed and free of fear. She was beautiful when she

was asleep.
Her slightly parted lips were paler than they should've been, but they were full. Her dark eyebrows arched attractively, and her nose was small and feminine. Her thick, dark hair didn't look so overwhelming when it was flipped to the side and laying harmlessly across the wooden floor beside her.

A man could tangle his fists in hair like that.

I turned back to the ceiling. Maybe I was hallucinating from shock. The adrenaline had done something uncomfortable to me. It hurt to move, but I felt fidgety like I must. I tried to sit up but realized I needed help to get anywhere. And stitches. Lots of stitches.

"Mira," I said.

She stirred. Her stomach growled again. She was starving, and I thought about Jake's Quickstop for the hundredth time in a week. She probably hadn't had groceries for a while because of me. I felt like grit.

I pulled my foot to the side and caressed her head with the tip of my boot. It was all I could do. "Mira, can you hear me?"

Her eyes fluttered behind her eyelids, and she opened them slowly. I couldn't look away. Her eyes weren't like everyone said.

Don't look into Crazy Mira's eyes. They'll pull you down to hell.

She'll cast her spell on you if you look into the black abyss of her eyes.

Her eyes weren't black. They weren't even dark. They were gray. My mind raced with the realization. Maybe I really was dreaming. Perhaps I was already dead. I squeezed my eyes shut. I couldn't be. Heaven wouldn't hurt this much, and I saw no hellfire.

As realization dawned on her face, her pupils began to dilate until her eyes looked black once again. A fear induced response then.

I looked back to the ceiling to give her privacy. "Mira, I think you need to eat something. Do you have anything to eat?"

She shook her head, her face scraping softly against the grain of the floorboard beneath it.

I clamped my teeth until my jawline worked. I'd never known hunger. Not like this. "Can you make it to the sink? Run the water and drink it until your stomach feels solid. It won't help for long but it might make you feel a little better until we can figure something out."

"Okay, I'll try. Don't look."

I turned my head to the wall, ignoring the pain in my neck. She scuffled to the kitchen and ran the water. She drank for a long time.

"Not too much or it'll make you sick," I advised.

The glass clinked on the counter. The sound of her boot steps faded, then returned as she came back to stand beside me.

"I'm dressed," she said.

She wore a thin gray tank top over her jean shorts. I couldn't take my eyes off a line of oddly puckered scars that ran in a circle around her throat. They stood out against her alabaster skin.

"What happened to your neck?" I asked.

She raised a hand to her chest in an attempt to cover them. Her face said she'd forgotten all about them. Her panicked gaze lifted back to the direction of the room she had come from. Her room.

"Do you have anything else to wear?" I asked, giving her an out.

She shook her head again. "Nothing that would cover them."

She looked longingly at the tattered rag against my neck.

"I owe you some new clothes then," I offered.

"I don't need your charity."

"It's not charity. One shirt for the shirt I ruined. Deal?"

She bit her lip. "Fine."

I tried again to sit up. "Where's your uncle? We need to send for a doctor while you start stitching up my neck."

"He's dead."

I stared at her dumbly. "Dead? Since when?"

The uncertain look on her face said she didn't know if she could trust me, but after a moment all I saw was resolve and wild hair. "Since last November."

I don't know what she saw on my face, but she scooted farther away from me and waited. I slid a suspicious gaze to the back room. What did I really know about Mira Fletcher? Only that every single person in town thought she was bat shit crazy. The kind of unbalanced that scares people. Who was I to argue with every single person who had come into contact with her in the last five years?

"Is he still in his room?" I asked in a low voice. My eyes held hers. I wanted the truth.

Her lip curled up in apparent disgust. "Yeah, I left his rotting corpse in his bed, Caleb. That is the creepiest thing anyone has ever said to me."

I cleared my throat, feeling bad for my earlier suspicions. "Where is he then?"

Her sigh tapered into a growl, and she stood to leave. I thought she was running from the confrontation, but she returned a minute later with a thick stack of papers in a manila envelope clenched in her shaking hand. She threw it on the floor in front of me and disappeared into her room.

The front of the baby-puke-colored folder had the words *Brady Fletcher's Will* written in angry, scribbled, dark letters. I unclasped the metal clips and pulled the stack of legal papers out. The first page was handwritten and signed by Mira's uncle at the bottom. An undignified piece of me found it surprising he'd been literate. I skimmed the document and grew bored enough on page two to toss them back onto the envelope. Mira returned with a stack of sheets in her arms.

"I buried him under the big oak tree out back like he wanted. He had the tombstone made years ago. I guess he lasted a lot longer than he thought he would. Or than he wanted. I don't know."

He had stated in his will he didn't want fuss. He had given Mira specific directions, and she had followed them. The law would question her about the timing, but I couldn't really find anything wrong with the way she put him to rest. "How did he go?"

"Drinking," was all she said.

Mira put her hands under my arms and dragged me as best she could with what little help I could offer. Other than my brain, my body didn't seem to want to work right. Mira said it was because I lost a lot of blood.

"You need a doctor," she said when I lay crumpled and broken on her bed.

"Why didn't you put me in your uncle's room? He won't need it."

"That room is haunted," she said matter of factly.

I chuckled, thinking she had made a joke, but she regarded me with serious eyes. Mira couldn't seem to take her gaze off of my curled lips. I wondered what she was thinking so I asked her.

"I haven't seen someone smile in a long time is all. You need a doctor," she repeated.

I sighed. I knew I did. The pain was excruciating, and I could feel the little blood I had left seeping out of my open neck. Open arms. Open chest. My skin felt cold except for the tiny puddle of fresh blood in the hollow of my neck. I tried not to swallow too hard for fear that my adam's apple would dislodge the only warmth I had left and loose the pool of firey liquid to flow down my throat and into Mira's clean sheets. I needed it more than they did.

"Do you know, you don't have a single gate in your fence line big enough for a truck? I had to borrow a horse from my dad's barn to get up here."

An antique looking chair screeched across the floor boards as she dragged it closer. Heavily, she sat. "That's the way my uncle wanted it."

"I won't live through another horse ride," I told her honestly. "It's gotta be you. You're going to have to put me back together. Do you have first aid?"

I expected her to pass out. Or to scream and clutch her chest, or I don't know, a hundred other reactions that any girl in town would've had. Instead, she nodded and disappeared to rustle through what sounded like a drawer full of supplies. She returned and dropped a needle into some peroxide before threading it deftly with a package of sterile sutures.

I arched my eyebrows in surprise. "Have you done this before? Given someone stitches?"

Mira tied a knot in the end and nodded.

"Who?"

"I've stitched myself. Now hold still," she said as she pinched the skin on my neck together firmly.

I gasped at the pain and squeezed my eyes as tightly shut as I could in hopes that it would help. It didn't. I tried to imagine Mira having to do this to herself but I couldn't wrap my head around it. The pain made me dizzy, and I focused on breathing. Breathe in, breathe out, two stitches down, breathe in, breathe out, another two stitches down. Only a billion more to go if Mira was ever to put Humpty Dumbass, the horseback-riding bear victim, back together again.

It took her two days to sew me back together. That's what it felt like at least. I waited to pass out from the pain, blood loss, and exhaustion, but I stayed miserably awake. I supposed it was my penance for hurting the girl who was working to save me. I watched her stitch the inside of my arm. I couldn't move my jaw much with the fresh sutures, but the top of her head bent over my body in concentration, moving only when she wiped more blood away from her work. I didn't understand how I had so much. How I was even still here, breathing.

I watched a bead of sweat run down the side of her face. It moved as if in slow motion, desperate to seek refuge in the wooden floor boards beneath her feet. To fall with a tiny moist sound to the earth, as drained of energy as I felt. I stared at it until a soft sigh escaped Mira's lips, and she straightened up, stretching her back. She wiped her face, and the bead of sweat became a small moist smear on the back of her hand, never realizing its goal.

"Done?" I asked in a gravelly voice I barely recognized as my own.

She seemed startled by the sound, and her eyes turned black. She scooted her chair farther away from me and looked at the ground. "It's the best I could do. I'm out of thread. The rest will have to heal, but you'll scar. Or maybe not. I don't know how it works for your kind."

My kind? "We can match," I said with a smile that held no humor. I don't know why I said that. I could tell me knowing about the marks around her neck made her uncomfortable, but my mouth just kept bringing them up. A part of me wished she would just tell me about them already.

She remained silent, too angry or afraid to meet my eyes. Instead, she looked at my chest and abdomen. Her gaze dragged slowly, and I wondered if she liked what she saw. Would a wild and fiercely independent creature such as Mira Fletcher ever look at a man intimately? From the way she stared unashamedly at my body, I thought maybe she wouldn't ever need a man. Not in the way a town girl like Becca Barns, who'd harbored a crush on me since the tenth grade, would need a man to coddle her, compliment her, and protect her.

"I need to go hunt," Mira said. "We both need to eat." She looked shaky and weak, but she stood with a fierce determination. A rifle clicked as she cocked it in the front room.

And just like that, she had answered my question.

Mira didn't need anyone.

****

Mira

Caleb McCreedy looked a lot better than any man I'd seen in the three Seventeen magazines I had read in one of my foster homes when I was a kid. I put my left hand over my cheek to feel if the skin there was growing hot at the memory of Caleb's shirtless chest. It was still cool to the touch. My body was apparently too hungry to waste energy on blushing.

No amount of filth or injury or blood could hide that Caleb was fit. Not the rail thin, emaciated look that I had unwillingly adopted in recent years, but the protein and veggies and heavy lifting kind of fit. His chest had flexed with every breath and every flinch of pain, and rippling mounds of muscle across his taut stomach begged for me to touch them, just to see if he was as hard as he looked. Shadows had hovered in the twin creases that dove over his hips and into his jeans, highlighting the light hair that trailed from his belly button down. Thank goodness I hadn't noticed that before I was done stitching him up or I would have never finished. Instead, I would've been petting him like a handsy lunatic.

For some reason I couldn't understand, the way he looked made me sad. Another beautiful thing I would never touch without it breaking or shuddering. He was a colorful glass-paned window in my black and white existence, and if I dared touch him, the shards would surely cut me deeper than any unkind words ever had. A man like him would never, ever want anything to do with a girl like me.

I knew all about Caleb, his brothers, sisters, and their father, an oil tycoon. Uncle Brady used to talk about them. They were the only family with real money in our sleepy little town. Caleb and I were unarguably from two completely different universes. That much had

been made clear with his words at Jake's Quickstop.
There was no room for someone like me in his world.
I was alien.
Searching the canopy above me for squirrels was the only thing that could pull me out of my revelry now.
There really was no use in mourning the loss of something that had never been mine to begin with.

Chapter Five
Caleb

I dreamt of the grizzly. It's glowing eyes held me in the night, as time after time I tried to get away, only to be swatted down again. My horse kept his attention. He was only playing with me. The predator had decided right away that I was no threat. What weapons did a puny human have against a bear? Stubbed nails and blunt teeth.

The grizzly hadn't counted on Mira, though. All she had were weapons. Mira's face came to mind and melded with the face of the bear. Wild black hair, black eyes, and two inch long canines that glistened as she screamed.

I lurched upward and yelped in pain. My skin was slick with sweat, and I huffed as if I had just run a marathon.

Mira had frozen in the chair beside the bed. It seemed she had been relaxed and unbothered by my unconscious presence. She lay sideways, one of her legs dangling over the arm and the other pressing bare toes into the railing of the old iron headboard of the bed. She had a textbook in her lap, and a pencil had stopped mid twirl between her fingers. Her other hand held a leafy green up to her mouth, and she nibbled at it like a startled rabbit.

My hair had fallen into my face, and I ran my fingers through it to smooth it back. She leaned forward and handed me a bowl off the floor. It smelled delicious. Inside were three small pieces of meat over some leaves I didn't recognize. Wait. I could identify two wild onions that stuck out of my bowl like a pair of chopsticks. One point for

McCreedy.

"Are you a witch?" I asked without thinking, afraid to eat the food after such a disturbing dream.

Mira was quiet for a while before she answered. "Is that what everyone says about me?"

She seemed to take my lack of answer as a "yes," snorted, and then pulled her hand over her mouth to cover her embarrassment. And then she squeaked and peeled into a tinkling giggle. "I'm sorry. I know you're serious, but it's just the most ridiculous question." She cleared her throat and tried to look severe. "No, I'm not a witch. But I wish I was so I could conjure some more food."

I felt stupid for asking. Wrapping a piece of meat into some of the greens, I took a cautious bite. It may have been that I was starving, but that small bite of food was one of the better tasting things I'd ever put into my mouth. I didn't even ask what kind of meat it was. I didn't want to know. "What are you studying?"

"Calculus," she said. "I hate it, but I have a test over in Mineral Wells in two weeks."

"Test for what?"

"I'm taking my GED. I'm getting my high school diploma. It's a little late, I know, but I had trouble finishing school after my uncle took me out."

"Did your uncle homeschool you?"

"He ordered the books once but never taught me anything. He just did it to get the state off his back in a pinch. For a while, I ordered the books and sent everything in like he was teaching me, but I couldn't afford it after that first year. In a couple of weeks, I'll be totally done, though."

She smiled with pride, and I was captured by it. Such a small gesture. The kind a person did a hundred times a day without realizing it. Mira never did. It made the smiles she gave that much more valuable.

My bowl was empty. My fingers had been feeling around and found nothing but the wild onions. I must have eaten the rest without realizing it.

"We need to figure out a way to get you to a doctor," she said, her eyes on the heat across my shoulders.

"Do you have a phone?" I asked hopefully.

"Nope." She made a popping noise at the end of the word. "Generator went out a while back. No power."

I frowned. Not because of the lack of a phone line, but because she had been living all alone without power. "Cell phone?"

She looked at me dubiously, and I grinned.

I said, "Never hurts to try."

She tapped her pencil against the side of her cheek and looked off into space. "I have a truck hidden outside of the fence. It was my uncle's. We'd still have to walk or take a horse over about forty acres to get to it, though."

Leaning back, I linked my hands behind my head. The movement pulled on sore stitches but my muscles felt good to stretch. It wasn't much of a choice, but sooner rather than later, people would start looking for me, and Mira didn't need any more trouble. I had to get out of here for the good of both of us.

"Okay," I said, "let's do it quick then."

Mira handed me a full glass of water. "I'll go get the guns. Bears hunt in pairs."

She disappeared out of the room, and my veins went cold, freezing me into place.

Mira popped her head back in through the doorway with a mischievous grin. "That was a joke."

I couldn't find a smile to encourage such behavior but she didn't seem to care and flitted off to saddle a horse. Her teasing wasn't funny for a full two minutes before I gave a quiet and private laugh. "Ha," I chuckled, amazed at the idea that Crazy Mira just told me a joke. The old ladies at Jake's would crap their pants if they ever got their hands on that information.

They wouldn't, though. That joke was only for me, and I'd keep it in my pocket, safe and warm and mine.

Before we left, Mira handed me a shot glass overflowing with whiskey. "No pain killers," she informed me.

I told her, "Whiskey'll do," and downed the liquor neatly. I hissed as the cheap, amber liquid seared down my throat.

Riding a horse in my condition was comparable to getting hit by a mac truck repeatedly. My body felt like the strips at the bottom of a paper shredder, and I wanted to curse at every bouncy step the old horse took. The brown horse Mira had brought up to the house was named Blue and was the oldest, most ill-bred horse I'd ever seen in my entire life. It was no small miracle it could walk, much less carry me. It followed Mira without prodding, though, and the reins lay slack and manageable in her hands as she led us to the truck. It was obvious the horse loved Mira and the feeling was mutual. She talked to the animal as if I weren't even here. Whether her chatter was habit from being lonely, or from something more unsettling, I couldn't tell.

"What can I do to repay you?" I asked, desperate for something other than the painful ride to focus on.

"Live. I don't want you on my conscience," she said shortly.

"That's not enough. What do you need? Just tell me, and I'll leave you alone about it."

Mira growled and kicked a rock with the toe of her boot. "Dammit, Caleb. I don't want anything."

The saddle horn creaked under my weight. It felt better if I was leaning forward. "Stop being so stubborn, Mira. I have a debt to repay you so let's just get it over with and then you can be done with me."

She was quiet for so long, I thought she was refusing to talk to me anymore.

"The house could use some repairs," she said over her shoulder.

"Done," I said. "I work the early shift on the rig every day but Sunday. I'll come over to the house when I have time off."

"Okay." She said it like she didn't expect to ever see me again, and I wondered if anyone had ever followed through with anything in her entire life.

"Caleb?" she asked, pulling Blue to a stop. Her eyes were wide and frightened looking.

"Yeah?"

"You're going to be different now."

I leaned back a little and shook my head in bafflement. Sure, I felt different about her. She couldn't know that, though. "I don't know what you mean."

She took a long drag of air and dropped her gaze to my work boot that rested in the stirrup. "The bear that did this to you wasn't just an animal. He was a man, too."

I waited for her to tell me she was just kidding, like she'd done earlier, but she just stood there, waiting for…something.

"Mira, that thing wasn't a man. I think I'd know if I was clawed and bitten and tortured by a man or a bear. I spent all night with the damned thing."

"He was a shifter. A bear man. He maybe should've killed you."

"What are you saying?" My voice sounded harsh, even to my own ears, but so what? "You wish I was dead? Then why did you just say you wanted me to live? Why did you save me?"

"I don't wish you were dead." Her voice dipped to a whisper. "You'll wish you were dead, and maybe you'll hate me for bringing you back."

There it was. That was the sign I'd been looking for. After all, the entire town couldn't have been wrong about her. She was as crazy as her uncle. I wanted to yell at her. To tell her the things she was saying weren't real. That she'd made them up as a coping mechanism for her loneliness or whatever else was going on in that head of hers. But when I opened my mouth to fling my angry words at her, the only thing that came out was a helpless sound.

I was disappointed. There. I was fucking disappointed, okay? Something in me had reached out for Mira at Jake's the other day, and I hadn't been able to stop thinking about her since. Then I'd spent some time with her and realized she was a decent person, and I wanted her to be okay.

But she wasn't.

And no amount of kindness from me was going to fix her.

"Okay, Mira. When I start feeling different, I'll let you know."

****

Mira

Today had been one of the best and one of the worst days of my life. The best because I had actually had a conversation with another human being who didn't make the devil horns at me, and the worst because Clancy Clayborn, the town sheriff, and one of his deputies I didn't recognize, pulled up in a patrol car at almost the exact same time we reached the truck. One look at Caleb, who looked like a murder victim, and they instantaneously decided I was his assassin.

"Hands up in the air where I can see 'em!" Clancy yelled at me, training his firearm directly at my face.

I dropped Blue's reins and did as he commanded. Then I was down on my knees, and down on my belly, and then I was being frisked by a cop with some serious body odor and three too many Jake's fried burritos in his paunch.

I couldn't hear what Caleb was yelling over the cop's loud directions, but he sounded furious. Up until the point when he passed out cold and fell in a crumpled heap onto the ground beneath Blue.

"Way to go, Nancy!" I yelled at Clancy from my vantage point in the dirt. "Now you killed him!"

Clancy and I were old not-friends. He was notorious for running me out of town for disturbing the peace when I wasn't doing anything but getting supplies. "Gotta keep the streets clean," he would say, then wipe his hands like he had done his civic duty. What a canker sore.

"Quiet, Crazy Mira," he ordered, his face going an interesting shade of mauve-purple in his rage. "Get her in handcuffs and tie up that horse," he told his deputy. "I'm gonna radio for backup. I have to get the McCreedy boy to the clinic." Clancy was already dragging Caleb's limp body toward the patrol car.

I was pretty sure a whole lot of police bylaws were being broken here, and from the shocked look on deputy-what's-his-name's face, he probably felt the same.

Clancy peeled out, throwing gravel and dust over where I lay. "You're so lucky to have such a rock solid boss," I sniped at the deputy. It wasn't characteristic of me to feel so brave and mouthy, but I was pissed.

He didn't look amused. "You know you have the right to remain silent, don't you?"

I plopped my head to the side. A rock dug into my cheek, but it was bearable. "Fine."

We waited for our ride to arrive ten minutes later in the form of the second and only other patrol car in Bryson.

A leisurely drive down Main Street in my snazzy ride was the cherry on top of the day. Apparently, every single person in town had already heard of my arrest and was waiting excitedly to see the crazy parade, party of one. A piece of me was surprised they weren't selling peanuts and cotton candy. I tried to slouch down as far as I possibly could with my hands cuffed much too tightly behind my back. I'm sure everyone could still see the top of my hair. It was all they needed. They'd talk about this for the rest of my life. They'd talk about it for the rest of their lives. Perhaps I would even get a book of my own in the town history section of the library.

"The Chronicles of Crazy Mira."

I feigned unbalance when they booked me. They asked less questions if I smiled and stared blankly at the wall. I even swayed and hummed off-key for good measure.

After an hour of no response about the unfortunate happenings to Caleb McCreedy, Clancy gave up and sent his deputy in to play good cop. The deputy, Young, Clancy had called him, cleared his throat as they passed each other in the doorway. Two substantial bellies tried to fit through the frame simultaneously, like two round moons orbiting each other. I wondered how many times they had done that dance to do it so well.

"The clinic just called. Caleb's awake," Young said in a low voice, just loud enough for me to catch it.

I perked up at the new information. Caleb wasn't dead then. A weight lifted, and I drew a long shaky breath. When I exhaled, some of the tension left my body with it. I was still in trouble up to my eyeballs, but at least Caleb would be all right.

Young opened his mouth to speak, but I interrupted him. "I think I need to talk to Sam Burns now."

"The lawyer?" he asked, obviously surprised that I could speak civilly *and* drop a useful name.

I had only met Sam Burns once before. I had gone into town with Uncle Brady on one of the rare occasions he thought it pertinent for me to be there. I liked the town lawyer's office. He had taken the effort to invest in an old-fashioned popcorn machine with white paper baggies clipped to the side. *Free to clients*, the sign over the front had read. I had filled my bag three times while Uncle Brady went over his will with the statuesque lawyer. It was all I had to eat that day, and was such a delicious and unexpected treat that I would forever hold Mr. Burns in a warm place in my heart. He couldn't have realized he'd made such a memory for me. I'd be lucky if he remembered me at all, but surely he would recall Uncle Brady. My guardian had been too loud a character to be forgotten easily.

I made the phone call, using the number I'd memorized from Uncle Brady's will. "Mr. Burns," I said when he answered. "This is Mira Fletcher, Brady Fletcher's niece. I'm being held at the police station and need your assistance."

His reply was simple. "I'll be there in twenty minutes."

I tried to be polite and say bye, but he'd already hung up.

Twenty minutes later and Mr. Burns was as I remembered him, except for not quite so tall and a little grayer around the edges. His eyes were sharp, and he seemed to take in everything with a single glance when he entered the room. "Hello again, Mira," he said kindly. The metal chair screeched across the tile floor, and he set a very professional looking briefcase on the table between us. It appeared downright odd against his T-shirt and worn blue jeans, but small town lawyers didn't have to dress up.

Without further ado, I got down to the nitty gritty of why I'd called him. "I have information regarding my uncle. First, I will need you to retrieve the satchel I had with me when I was arrested. It had paperwork pertinent to what I need from you."

"Yes, all right," he said.

His tone sounded as if he were talking to a child. I ignored it. My popcorn memory wavered, but I clutched onto it tighter.

He returned with my worn canvas bag about five minutes later, and I pulled out my uncle's will. "My uncle has passed," I said.

Burns's face showed little surprise. "When did it happen?"

"Almost a year ago."

His eyebrows shot up. "What? Why haven't you told anyone, child?"

I glared at him for the last comment. "Well, I thought you could help me explain." I pushed my uncle's handwritten will across the table, and Burn's pulled out a pair of reading glasses before he opened the oversized envelope.

"I see," he said thoughtfully after he was finished reading the first scribbled page. "I am to assume you have done as he requested and buried him where he specified?"

"Exactly where. He went over and over it with me."

"Do you understand the rest of the will he had drawn up?" he asked.

I shook my head. I had tried to read it a few times, but all of the legal mumbo jumbo made it difficult for me to understand. Sometimes when I was tired and couldn't sleep, I read it knowing full-well I'd pass out by section two, but I wouldn't tell Mr. Burns how boring his writing was. I had manners, after all.

Burns thumbed through the copy of the paperwork he'd drawn up. "Basically, your uncle has left the two hundred acres of your family's land in your name, claimable upon your eighteenth birthday. Which is when? If you don't mind me asking."

"Two years ago today."

His eyes went round. "We will have paperwork to sign back at my office then. I have to tell you one odd request he had. You will be unable to sell the land for a minimum of one decade, or ten years."

A lump swelled in my throat, making it hard to swallow, much less breathe. I would be stuck in that haunted house for another ten years of my life. I wasn't finishing my sentence there. I was only beginning it. I clenched my hands together under the table. My uncle had been kind enough to give me a home, and then cruel enough to drown me with it.

"The police will have questions about his passing. How did he go?"

"In a pool of vomit on his bathroom floor. He drank himself to death, sir," I said, void of emotion. I had tried so hard to say the sentence without reliving the horrific scene on the cold morning I had found him.

The sharp inhale of breath from the lawyer told me my reaction to the question wasn't normal. But then again, what about me was?

"I'm sorry," he said. He opened his mouth to say more but couldn't seem to find the words he wanted.

Trying to avoid thinking of the morning Uncle Brady had died proved fruitless. After Burns talked privately with Clancy and Young, they grilled me for every detail of the day my uncle had passed. I was raw and vulnerable after having to share so much of such a terrifying and private experience. It was the first time I had said the words out loud or talked to anyone about it, and the admission hurt more than I thought it would.

"You're free to go," Clancy said ungraciously after I had worn my voice thin talking.

"I am?"

"Caleb woke up and explained that you were trying to save him. The doctor confirmed it was a bear attack," Young explained.

I stood to leave, and Burns opened the door for me.

35

Clancy's voice sounded harassed behind me. "Don't leave town, Miss Fletcher. We'll still be investigating your uncle's death and the reasons you waited a *year* to tell us."

"Don't worry," I said, sounding tired and sad, even to myself. "It seems I'll be stuck here forever."

Clancy didn't look any happier about it than I was, and I thought of Bora Bora for the hundredth time tonight.

"I don't have much money, Mr. Burns. What do I owe you for everything?" I asked as we stopped by the front door to the small police station.

"Absolutely nothing. Your uncle already paid me to set up his will and make sure it was carried out. You have done most of the work for me." He started to leave but turned back around. "Mira, I think I should be present if the police question you about your uncle. Please call me if they do."

The clinic where Caleb was being treated was just down the street, but it might as well have been a million miles away. I stepped out into the dark. Clouds blocked out the moon and stars and cast shadows over everything. Fitting for my mood. I began the long walk alone, and when the streetlights ended, I pressed the sad memories of Uncle Brady's death back where they belonged.

****

Caleb

A hundred people and no one came to visit me in the clinic.

Nearly the entire town had turned out, and it left me exhausted. Humbled and appreciative, but by the time the last of the visitors left on the third day, I needed a vacation from bed rest. Everyone visited, but I didn't feel any connection as I received their well-wishes and thoughtful cards.

Sure, I smiled, shook hands, and laughed at jokes, but my eyes were drawn to the door and my mind distracted. I could lie to myself and say I sought escape, but what my searching eyes really wanted was the silhouette of someone I knew would never—could never—visit me here.

A hundred people and no one came.

Chapter Six
Mira

Desperation and weakness was going to send me scuttling back into town for the second time in as many days.

Metal and paper flopped into the palm of my hand as I upended Uncle Brady's coffee can. He hadn't believed in the integrity of banks. Every penny he made, he stuffed in the can.

I had learned my lesson last week, and I wasn't going to take any chances at a repeat experience. I would get to Jake's Quickstop at ten in the morning after most were at work and before many were on a break for lunch. There would still be people. That was unavoidable as there were always people at Jake's Quickstop, but I could limit my risks. I looked at my list with a critical eye. The total cost should be well below what I was bringing, but I marked *eggs* off just to be certain.

We used to have chickens. Red and brown mottled things that kept us with fresh eggs every morning. They would stay close to the house in hopes of food, a continuous cluck deep in their throats. It was a soft sound that had become a part of my daily soundtrack. The oldest stopped producing, and the eggs dwindled to nothing. When there were no more to be had, I had cooked the chickens. Desperate times and measures and all. The rooster had been the last to go. He was mean as sin, but I had liked him. Silence had replaced their music and made the place feel too quiet. Too lonely.

I had tried to buy new chickens from one of the local farmers. He had refused me because his wife thought I would bring bad luck on their home and crops if he did business with me. It was the first and last time I tried to purchase anything outside of Jake's Quickstop. Bernard wasn't a Mira-fan, but he didn't make the sign of the cross when I entered his store, and he charged me fairly. That was good enough for me.

I shoved the money in my pocket and headed for the barn. I liked to call it a barn, but it was really just a rough half-room with a partial roof to shelter the horses at the edge of their corral. Once Bobby was saddled, we headed down the trail that would lead us to the truck.

The truck was called the Green Monster, and rightly so. It was a Ford, and old, and had originally been purchased by my grandfather to help with work on the acreage that had been passed down from his father and his father's father before him. My grandfather had been well-liked in town. The crazy didn't start seeping through the limbs of our family tree until Uncle Brady's generation.

It had been my uncle's bright idea to fence in the gates and make our land impassible by vehicle. He did it right after the adoption officials started arriving regularly, and his plan worked. Hiking out to Narnia wasn't an attractive option for most underpaid social workers with stacks of paperwork, sketchy cell phone reception, too many kids to keep up with, and high heels. So to go into town, I had to get creative and stash the truck just outside our property line.

The places that weren't rusted on the truck were colored an attractive pastel green. I loved it, even with all of its imperfections. No one in the world could get it started but me. There were nine tricks to getting that old engine to turn over, and I could do them all without even thinking.

I tied off the horse and hopped into the unlocked truck. I never worried about someone stealing it. They wouldn't be able to start it, and if they did get the idea to hotwire the beast, The Green Monster would still demand five more tricks be performed before it graced them with first gear.

I rolled down the window as I hit the edge of the dirt road to better flip off the green sign that identified my street. Who in their right mind would name a street Dark Corner Road besides the devil himself? I was pretty sure it's where the witch rumors had originated.

To keep my hands from shaking, I clenched the wheel until my knuckles were white. Every mile that brought me closer to town terrified me a little more. It was always like this. I tried to talk to myself to calm my nerves, but the tremble in my voice annoyed me and made me feel weaker than I already did. Caleb's face flickered across my mind, and my hands relaxed. He was in town. I was sure of it. He'd have to stay at the clinic for a while with injuries as bad as his. That was if they hadn't shipped him off to a fancy hospital in the city. The thought made me nervous again. It wasn't like I would get to see him. The thought of visiting him in the clinic with all of those people around was terror-inducing.

I pushed the gas down with the tips of my toes. I just wanted to get this over with.

I'd always loathed the bell above the door at Jake's Quickstop. Pushing the door open as softly as I could never helped. If anything, it made it louder, but I always tried, anyway. Bernard glared at me as I slid through the barely open door. Still mad, then.

I glanced up to see two small groups of people sitting near the dining area. I puffed a little sigh of relief and grabbed a shopping basket.

I could hear everything they said. Not on purpose. I hated eavesdropping, but in an ironic twist of fate, I had been born with superior hearing. Sometimes, I wished I couldn't hear at all. Nobody talked to me, anyway.

"I heard she cooked old man Fletcher up for dinner and saved his bones for soup," a girl around my age said to her two friends in a whisper-yell.

"Well, I heard he isn't dead at all and that Caleb McCreedy was out there investigating. And that's when she sicced her pet bear on him so he wouldn't find out she'd been torturing her uncle all this time," another one said.

I pretended I didn't hear them and that their words didn't sting. "Where's the damned peanut butter," I grumbled, impatient for my escape.

Everyone quieted at the sound of my voice, and I barely avoided my legs locking up on me. Stupid trembling hands.

Something landed with a splat against my ankle. All six people at the tables snickered, so I couldn't begin to guess who threw it. I pulled a soggy noodle off my leg and looked around for somewhere to put it. Everyone laughed harder—probably because I looked like I was glaring at the soup cans for someone to blame. Hanging the fettuccini over the side of my basket, I finished my shopping and headed for the front. Every step brought relief because I was farther away from my tormentors.

Bernard rang up the groceries and bagged them as I counted out exact change. He'd never before talked to me other than what was necessary to exchange goods and money, so I jumped when he said my name.

"Yes?" I sounded terrified and small.

"I'm sorry about your uncle."

"Yeah," one of the girls from the back chimed in. "Now you're all out of family to eat." She and her friends peeled into laughter.

"Eat your food and let her be," Bernard snapped.

His voice was loud and commanding, and it scared me. I tried to smile my thanks to him, but it came out as a lip tremble instead, and I scurried out of Jake's before anyone said anything else.

I clutched onto my single bag of groceries and looked down the street. I don't know why. I always went straight for my truck with my head down, but for some reason I couldn't help looking for Caleb. In the daylight, I could see the sterile looking clinic with its whitewashed brick. Despite my panic, I moved down the sidewalk to my left. What would I say to him? The last time I'd spoken to him, it was obvious he thought I was insane for talking about bear men. Would he throw me out? How many people would be visiting him? He was a McCreedy after all, so of course there would be visitors.

A loop of horrifying questions ran through my mind until I reached for the front door of the clinic. I was surprised when the door opened suddenly from the inside. Unable to pull my hand away quickly enough, it jammed against the unforgiving metal, making a deep *thunk* sound and sending pain shooting straight up my arm from where my wrist had overextended.

Hooking the groceries with an arm, I held the hurt part with my other hand like the pressure would make it feel better. I'd had much worse, but the pain was unexpected.

A girl my age appeared out of the doorway. She was wiping her eyes with a tissue, and her nose looked red from crying. Big blue eyes, light brown hair, and lightly freckled skin told me she was pretty, and I felt sad that she was leaving in tears. Maybe she had lost someone, too.

"Mira," she said in a harsh voice. "Is it true that you stitched up Caleb McCreedy after that bear attack?"

My eyes went wide at being talked to directly. I shifted my weight from side to side and tried to peel my gaze from her angry face.

"Well?" she demanded so loudly I jumped and shrank into myself.

"Yes," I whispered.

Her look darkened. "You only stitched up half of what needed to be done, and poorly at that. His body is ruined now." Hate tainted every word. "He will be scarred for life, and everyone will look at his skin out of pity. Because of you."

A shorter girl beside her put a gentle hand over her forearm. "Becca," she said, looking around at the gathering crowd. "I think we should go."

Becca shoved by me, bumping my shoulder and spinning me to the side as she passed. I stared after her in disbelief and confusion. I hadn't made those scars on Caleb. The grizzly had. No, Mr. Idiot Shifter Eli Emmerson had, for reasons I hadn't a guess at. I had only tried to help, and I had done the best I could. I'd thought about it over and over and couldn't imagine a way I could have done it differently—done it better. I wished I had the balls to say those things out loud to her and defend myself.

Suddenly, I was angry at Caleb. Why had he been up on my land, anyway? He wouldn't have been attacked if he would have been back at his big safe mansion with the rest of his snooty family. And he'd still be fucking human! And now I carried all this guilt, and apparently the blame, too.

His fault.

I glared at a familiar, dark-headed man who had come too close and pushed past the murmuring crowd. I peeled out of town as fast as my truck could go—which was actually really slow and anticlimactic.

When I was younger, I had this foster family I liked. I had been passed around a lot and labeled a problem child because I didn't talk very much and I looked funny. Something about me didn't sit well with people who didn't understand what I'd been through. This one family though, the Millers, had a biological son who was bad news. He would destroy anything he could get his hands on, and he would always blame it on me because he knew I wouldn't defend myself. Life was pretty miserable until the Millers decided they didn't believe him anymore, so they would ask me if he was telling the truth, and a funny thing happened. For the first time in my life, someone believed me. I never told them, but I had prayed every night that they would adopt me. It was the only time I had ever wanted such a whimsical thing. When a social worker came to take me away from the Millers, my heart had shattered into a million tiny pieces, like one of the fine china plates their son had thrown against the edge of a table in a tantrum. It hadn't mattered how honest I was, they still hadn't wanted me. Hadn't cared.

"Learn your lesson, Mira," I growled at myself.

Sticks and stones would break my bones, but frivolous wishes would break my heart.

****

Caleb

I fell out of bed in the dark, drowning, suffocating, and burning from the inside out. Every inch of my skin felt washed in live embers. Short bursts of breath squeezed from my lungs as I kicked out of the covers that had ensnared my legs.

Something was happening. Something inside.

I tried to yell out in pain, but a snarling sound rippled from my throat as I stumbled for the bathroom. The light was blinding, like my eyes were oversensitive. My vision was humming with small pulses that made everything look crisp, then blurry again. Gripping either side of the sink, I lifted my eyes to the mirror and shook my head in horror at what I saw there.

My eyes. I leaned closer and ran my trembling fingers across my cheek. The color was supposed to be blue, but instead, they were gold on the outside, glowing like the freaking sun, and green on the inside. I didn't understand. Fighting for air, I searched the medicine cabinet for anything that would explain this away. I had to be hallucinating as a side-effect from the pain meds the clinic had prescribed me.

Panicked, I yanked all of the bottles of Advil and vitamins out until they all clattered across the sink, then jerked the orange bottle of pain pills to my face. Holy shit. I could see the individual paper fibers the label had been made with. *Focus.*

Nausea, drowsiness, dizziness, fatigue, headache, skin rash, and not a damned word about hallucinations.

"Oww." The word tapered into a gravelly voice that couldn't belong to me. Pin pricks shot from my lips and cheeks, and when I looked into the mirror again, I had short, blunt whiskers and my face was beginning to morph into something I didn't recognize.

I needed help. No! I couldn't tell anyone about this. I ran for the front door, needing to do something, but at a loss on how to fix my broken self. I threw it open and let the wind caress my bare chest. I dragged lungful after lungful of fresh air into me and tried to think.

Who would believe me?

Who would believe I was this monster now?

Mira.

My eyes were drawn to the woods. I'd bought Eli's place a while back and was on the property beside Fletcher land now.

If I could get to her, she could help me. She knew. She'd tried to warn me about what I would become, and I hadn't believed her. She wasn't crazy. She was the only person in this whole damned town who knew what was real.

I grunted as pain rippled up my spine and bent me forward. On all fours, I closed my eyes as the agony became blinding. I screamed as my skin felt like it exploded, casting me upward with the force of my transformation. I landed heavily on all fours, hard enough to rock the porch.

My paws were huge, and six-inch black claws made marks across the wood floor as I shifted my weight. Thick, dark fur covered my arms and chest. When I turned to look at my reflection in the window, I wanted to run. Staring back at me with gold-rimmed, bottomless eyes was a fully matured grizzly bear. I was no longer me, but *other*. I was one of those bear men Mira had whispered about the day she'd saved me.

I sat heavily, completely out of control of my new body. I wanted so badly to go back an hour ago when I'd been sleeping comfortably in my bed, thinking I was going to be okay. I wasn't going to be okay at all. This wasn't just some weird hobby or embarrassing pastime. This was something I would have to hide from everyone I knew and loved to protect them, and to protect me.

A low rumble rattled my throat and I tried to imagine what my family would say if they saw me like this.

I had to hide what I was now from everyone.

Everyone but Mira.

Heaving upward again, I stood and managed to spread all of my paws wide enough to stay upright. I swayed as I tried to realize my new balance.

My heart was pounding against my ribcage. I could hear it. I could hear everything. Leaves fluttering in the soft breeze all the way from the tree line. Some small mammal scurried around the forest floor some distance off, and the soft call of bullfrogs sounded so loud it made the hairs of my ears tingle. The tall grass, swaying in the wind, jerked my attention with every shift. The old rocking chair behind me creaked, and I jumped away and growled. I growled! Ears flat, canines bared, and I made the sound of an animal at the movement of a harmless chair.

I made a shitty monster.

Get it together, Caleb. Looking down at my giant paws, the size of dinner plates, I flexed them. They made little scars on the wood beneath. I wasn't helpless. I wasn't human. Now, I was all weapons. Just like the grizzly—the bear man—who had tried to kill me. Or perhaps he was only trying to change me. But why?

Lowering my lips to cover my teeth, I lifted my senses back to the woods that stood between me and Mira's house. Some sick part of me wanted her to see me like this, like some apology for scoffing at her when she'd tried to warn me about my fate. I wanted her to know she'd been right, and that I was sorry—that I was wrong.

Maybe it was the panic and confusion talking, but suddenly, I wanted her to see me, and I wanted to see her more than anything.

With her face as my motivation, I took my first step in this new body, and then the second. By the time I'd reached the trees, I was able to trot. My breath sounded like panting that tapered into a soft growl as I gained confidence in my new form. Cool air blasted in front of me with every breath. Night birds called out from the canopy above, but quieted as I drew nearer, as if they could sense danger. Was I the danger? I must've been because I could make out the sound of field mice, their little heartbeats hammering as they scurried to their homes when I passed.

I began to run, testing the power in my new legs, and on a whim, I leaped through the air and landed with my claws in an old cottonwood tree. When I held, I widened my eyes at the claws dug deep into the bark and looked up into the branches. Bunching my muscles, I heaved upward until I reached the lowest branch. It wasn't thick enough to hold my weight, so I slid down, clawing the tree as I went, leaving long gashes in the bark. I looked at my claws, but they hadn't dulled a bit. A strange feeling spread through me. I'd loved climbing trees as a kid, but as I'd grown older, I'd fallen out of the habit. I'd lost the joy in it. The freedom. As I looked up into the branches, a little wisp of that joy came back. Maybe this wasn't all bad.

My ears twitched at a sound that echoed through the woods. It cracked again and picked up a steady rhythm. Curious, I trotted toward it.

I could smell her long before I could see her. Mira was chopping wood in the clearing in front of her house. Or trying to. Her arms were too thin, and she looked weak, but that didn't stop her from putting block after block on an old stump and hefting an ax down onto it. The blade was old and rust-eaten, and she could only manage to get it through the top few inches. Then, she'd pick up the ax again, still attached to the wood, and crack it down against the stump. It took her at least four swings to get one log split each time.

I didn't know how long I stood there, watching her, wanting to help but unable to. A great pity took me at how exhausted she was becoming, but a great pride surged through me at how determined she was to finish her chore. She was the strongest woman I'd ever met, and I'd only seen a fraction of her struggle.

She rested her hands on her knees, and from here, I could see her shaking at the elbows. The soft sound of her stomach growling drew me forward a step. She was hungry. I didn't know how I could fix it, but I wanted to.

Mira looked up with frightened, wide eyes as the wind shifted. Straightening, she scanned the woods around me. Her eyes never landed on me directly, but she began to back away as if she could sense my presence. As if she could sense me watching her.

I sank back deeper into the shadows and lowered my head. She was scared. I could smell the acrid scent of it on the breeze. It was me she feared, and disgust flooded my gut. I shouldn't have come here. I'd been wrong about being able to share this with Mira. What gave her immunity from the danger of my existence? I'd immediately decided to shield my family and friends from what I'd turned into, but not Mira.

Why?

Didn't she have enough on her plate just trying to survive?

I sank farther back into the woods as she ran for the front door and slammed it closed behind her. I imagined her clutching that little rifle she'd brought the day she saved me. I imagined her staring at the door in horror, waiting for someone, or something, to come in after her. Her breath trembling, hands shaking, arms weary as they lifted the rifle.

All because of me.

I didn't want to complicate her life. She was practically a stranger who'd taken a great risk saving my sorry hide. The best thing I could do for her was to hide this from her, too.

****

Mira

It had been a month since Caleb McCreedy. The weather had changed from the hot and blinding brightness of summer to the cool and dim promise of autumn. I had passed my final exams and was a high school graduate. There had been no party or graduation cards. Just me and Uncle Brady's mangy old dog, who had decided to show up after three months of me thinking he was dead in the woods somewhere. He would only stay around if there was a chance of a meal. There wasn't for either of us, so he'd be gone again to find something better before long.

I had taken up my favorite sleeping posture in the night sometime, curled up in a ball with my arms wrapped around my stomach. It eased the ache if I lay like this, and because of it, I'd slept like the dead.

A noise rattled the walls, and I lurched upward and covered my ears as they were assaulted by some sound I couldn't identify in the first moments of wakefulness. Screaming?

My breath was rushed as I looked around my room for something I could use as a weapon. The light bulb above me flickered and went out, and then flickered on and held.

My head swiveled frantically. "What's happening," I whispered.

The ghost of Uncle Brady had come back for me. That's what was happening.

I jumped up and got tangled in my bed sheets on my way off the bed. I fell to the floor and smacked my knees against the wooden planks below. One broke in half and dangled under my leg, held in place by two rusty nails that hadn't quite given up yet. Scrabbling for the door, I ran for the old record player in the living room, as it seemed that was where most of the sound was coming from. It was playing an old Elvis record at maximum volume. I yanked the cord out of the wall and yelped when I saw the kitchen.

Either someone had been in my house, or the magic grocery fairy had come a callin'.

Rows and rows of brown plastic Jake's Quickstop bags full of food lined the counters and table.

"Morning," came a deep voice from the doorway.

It was barely light outside, but I would be able to pick out Caleb's silhouette anywhere. He leaned up against the doorframe, and I swear I could see a smirk in his stance.

"What are you doing here?" I asked. My heart was pounding against my sternum so hard it hurt.

"Do you always sleep in that?" he asked, ignoring my question and pointing to my lack of pants.

My one pair of shorts was flapping around in the breeze to dry outside, so it had been a tank top and undies kind of night for me.

My hands rocketed to cover my front but Caleb was already walking toward the kitchen, apparently not giving a fig about my state of undress. He wore a tight fitting, gray, V-neck T-shirt and some baggy jeans with a utility belt full of tools slung low around his hips. His pants had dried paint and smudges of black on them and holes frayed with plain white strands of undyed denim at the knees. Work pants.

I should have left to put my shorts on, but I couldn't quite pull myself away from the sight of Caleb in my kitchen and the ripple of the muscles in his back as he tugged on...

"No! Don't open—"

He pulled on the refrigerator door, and the smell of the food that had been entombed for the past nine months wafted out like a stinky tidal wave.

"Oh, God." I gagged and covered my nose with the back of my hand as my eyes watered.

Caleb must have been holding his breath because he ignored the smell and went right to work on dumping the contents of the fridge into a large trash bag. I went and propped the front and back doors open in hopes that it would help some of the stink escape. Bolting, I yanked my shorts off the clothesline outside and shimmied into them. When I came back in, Caleb tossed me a plastic container of sanitary wipes and opened a can of his own.

"Fridge is working. We need to get it clean quick, though. The milk is getting warm." He stopped and looked critically at me. "On second thought, let me do this and you eat something. I can see every one of your ribs through your shirt."

The rows of grocery bags were enough to overwhelm me. "Why are you doing this?"

"Because you saved my life. Don't be stubborn. It's part of the debt. Just eat."

He had turned when he was talking, and I could see the red, angry scars the bear had made across his neck. He had them on his arms, as well, but the one on his neck was what held me. It tapered and disappeared under his shirt, and I wanted to see more. I took a step forward and reached my hand out to touch it. Caleb stood frozen, his face an unreadable mask, and I let my hand fall back to my side.

"Does it hurt?" I asked.

He sighed, and his face took on a hard and distant look. "Do yours?"

"Not until I see them in the mirror," I said honestly. He'd tried to hurt me by bringing up my scars, but I understood the instinct to use that kind of weapon. I searched for anything to ease his pain. "It gets better with time."

"That's hard to believe," he said, turning back to the fridge to wipe it down. "It's all anybody looks at anymore."

His internal struggle was so thick, it settled like a mist on my skin. Did he blame me, too? Did he think he looked that way because of me, like that Becca girl did?

"Can I ask you something?"

"What?" he asked in a gruff voice.

Four freshly killed fish had been dropped on my doorstep over the past month, and last I checked, that mangy old dog of mine wouldn't have ever bothered sharing his food with me. "Did you bring me the fish?"

His eyes narrowed, as if I was crazy. "What fish?"

"Oh. Never mind." Embarrassed, I dropped my gaze to his work boots until he went back to cleaning and released me from his impossibly blue gaze.

I rifled through a plastic bag, vowing to take the first thing that was edible and leave him to his work. A box of mixed berry granola bars caught my attention, and I opened it as fast as I could. My hands trembled, and my legs felt wobbly enough to knock my knees together.

"You want one?" I hadn't meant to whisper, but it was all that came out.

He stopped what he was doing and swiveled his head to me. "What's wrong?" he asked through a look of confusion.

I wouldn't risk speaking, so I shook my head and stared at the box of treasures I held clutched to my chest. Nothing was wrong—except that Caleb was marred because of me, and now he was in my kitchen paying back some stupid debt he didn't owe, and now I'd somehow pissed him off again. And he felt so big in my tiny home that it was hard to breathe. Strong and in control, he worked without trying to be quiet, and his strength seeped out of him when he shut drawers, set cans down, or closed the fridge. He was overwhelming. And beautiful. But mostly overwhelming.

I skittered back into my room, but I could feel his gaze follow me until the door clicked closed behind me. How could I explain what was wrong with me when my feelings were just a mass of confusion not even I was equipped to interpret?

One granola bar package sat on the bed beside me, and I guiltily ate a second. I wished I could eat up every single thing Caleb had brought, but I wasn't a dog. I knew about rationing. If I was careful, this food could last me two months. I peeked out the door to watch Caleb. He was putting cold things into the fridge with swift and confident accuracy. I shut the door again and sat on my bed like a coward, clutching onto the box of leftover granola bars as if it would get the wise idea to try and run away.

I didn't know this Caleb. He was strong, quick, overpowering and intimidating. He was a tornado, as beautiful as he was terrifying. This house had only known the weak and ravaged Caleb born of injury and pain.

A light knock on the door pulled me from my thoughts. Caleb opened it slowly and peered in. "Can we talk?"

He sat on the bed beside me before I figured out my answer. He was so close I was breathless, as if a bowling ball sat on top my chest. I stood and scurried into the small bathroom. He could talk all he wanted to, but I didn't have to listen from three inches away.

Caleb seemed undeterred. "I need your permission to widen a gate so I can get my truck up here. It's going to be the only way I can get the supplies I need up to the house."

"Like what supplies?" I asked around the foam created by my toothbrush.

"Like, lumber for one. Half this place is rotted and not fit to be living in."

I spat frothy mint into the sink. "That sounds expensive."

"Speaking of, that generator out back is working for now, but it won't last forever. You need electricity up here, Mira. You can't go through the winter with no heat. Is it as important to you as it was to your uncle to live off the grid?"

I frowned at my reflection. It was nice not answering to anyone or paying the bills, but my bones still ached when I thought about the end of the last chilly winter without that generator.

I spat again and rinsed my mouth. "No. That isn't important to me, but I don't have the money to pay an electrician."

"My older brother, Brian, will be out here first thing in the morning to tap you into a power line. I can't imagine it will take too much to heat this little house. Your fireplace works?"

I finished rinsing my face and gave him a thumbs up outside of the bathroom with one hand while I dried my face with the other.

"Good. A couple more space heaters, and you should be doing all right."

My head was whirling. Where would I get all of this magic money? I couldn't even afford food.

I had pulled my hair into a messy bun at the back of my head to dry my face. It felt good to have the weight off my neck, and I returned to my bedroom in the same fashion. I took a seat in the chair by the bed to avoid overly close contact with Caleb again. That felt too dangerous.

He stared, and in an astonished tone said, "You look different with your hair back."

"I'm sure you do, too," I countered, uncomfortable under the scrutiny. His hair was shoulder-length and long enough. He could almost get his hair into a stub of one, at least.

Caleb cleared his throat. "Anyway, doing all of this stuff is great and all, but you need a way to make a living. I don't have any stake in this, and you can ignore my suggestions, but I bet you could put a pump jack up here and find some oil. You are in prime oil country after all. You could make your land pay you."

I was startled. That was something I'd never in my life thought about, though I know a lot of people in town made money in some form from the oil industry.

"How do you know they would find oil on my land?" I asked.

"Well, I don't know if they will, but I… Look, don't freak out but I bought old Eli's place just west of your property line several months back."

I sat up straighter. "How could you buy his place so long ago? He just died last month." By my bullet, but I didn't like to dwell on stuff like that. The nightmares were enough.

Caleb sighed and leveled me a look that said he wished he could tell me everything that had ever been. "He went missing last year, and his place was already in default a couple years before that. I picked the land up cheap because nobody in town wanted to touch a property they said was haunted."

"Is it?" I asked.

"It is now." He said it quick but looked like he immediately regretted it.

I pushed before he shut down completely on me. "Do you think that's why he did it?"

"Who?"

"Eli Emmerson. Do you think he turned you because you own his land?"

"Like revenge?" he asked with a slight frown.

And that's all I needed to know. I couldn't help the triumphant look that stretched my face. That had been a test, and Caleb McCreedy had failed. "You're a bear shifter too now, aren't you?"

"Mira," he warned.

"Who am I going to tell?" I made a show of looking around. "These walls don't share my secrets, Caleb. You still human or not?"

His expression darkened, and he looked away, staring out the window like the woods outside were the most interesting sight on the planet. Fine. If he wasn't going to talk, he could listen.

"Eli's sons were killed by poachers. He told me and Uncle Brady about it. People in town think they just up and left for a different life somewhere, but they got shot up when they were running as bears out in the woods one night. Eli wasn't right after that. Even Uncle Brady called him crazy, and you've probably heard about how unstable he was. When you have a lunatic calling you a lunatic, you're a damned lunatic. And that's where Eli was headed. Maybe he felt like turning bear for good, or maybe you all go full bear when you get old and sick like he was. I don't know. But if he knew you were the new owner of his land, the land that has passed to the sons in his family for generations, maybe he wanted to punish you."

"It's not a punishment, Mira." Caleb had said it as softly as he possibly could. "I don't think he saw it like that. He bled me slow. Killing me would've been a punishment. That crazy old shifter thought he was giving me a gift."

"How do you know?"

Resting his elbows on his knees, he dropped his head and ran his hands through his hair roughly. "Because I think about it all the damned time, Mira. The way he tortured me…" Caleb swallowed hard. "The way he did it makes me think he was deliberately trying to turn me, not kill me. He had no sons left. He picked me to keep the monster alive."

"Do you think it's a gift?"

He jerked his head up, and I gasped at the gold-rimmed, inhuman eyes that met mine. An empty smile crooked his lips. "No, Mira. Seeing you fear me isn't a gift. Knowing what the town would do to me if they found out what I am isn't a gift. Eli Emmerson's last act on this earth was to curse me." He stood and gripped the knob on my bedroom door. He kept his eyes cast away from me to hide the unnatural color. "I put jacks up on my land and they are already paying. It won't be a permanent solution if it is one at all. You are going to have to find a job so you can live."

"I am living," I said defensively.

"Mira," he said, squeezing his eyes tightly closed. When he looked at me again, they were blue again. "This isn't living."

He reached into his pocket, then handed me a piece of crumpled paper. I read over it and tried to hide the disappointment from my face.

Don's Butcher Shop
May's Florist
Soft Time Linens
Library
Pizzeria

"I've already applied to all of these places," I said quietly. "Except for the butcher shop. The sign on his door said *now hiring* but when I tried, Mr. Don said he didn't have any openings." The rest of them had said different variations of the same thing. I'd be bad for business.

Caleb stared at me for a long time, then shook his head like I'd said something unbelievable. "Before we do anything to your place, we need to have the title squared away for you to give me permission to do the electric and open the gate wider. Is the deed in your name?"

"Uncle Brady's will put it in my name when I turned eighteen. I have to sign some paperwork with Mr. Burns before it's all official, though."

"Okay, get dressed," he said. "We need to go into town and get that taken care of before anything else."

"Right now?" I asked. Usually, I mentally prepared myself for a couple of days before a trip to Main Street.

"Yes, right now," he clipped out. "As soon as the clinic okays me, I'm going back to work on the rig. That gives us roughly two weeks to get this place in shape."

"Okay," I whispered, wanting badly not to disappoint him. "I'm ready."

"You're ready?" he asked incredulously.

I pulled the rubber band out of my hair and my dark locks slid back in front of my face. "I don't have anything else to wear," I admitted. I could feel my cheeks burning with the admission, but I stood my ground and stared his glorious eyes down.

His gaze faltered first, sliding down to rest on the ring of scars around my neck. His expression was unreadable, but he'd seen them before, so I didn't cover them up. He already knew I was damaged goods.

"Come here," he demanded quietly.

Part of me wanted to buckle against such a direct command, but a bigger part of me reveled in the sound of the deep authority in his voice. Caleb McCreedy was a capable man, and though I'd never admit it out loud, I trusted him.

I followed him into the kitchen where he began searching the plastic bags. I opened the fridge to see what it looked like to have a full icebox. It was a scene from a dream. Except…

"Caleb?"

"Hmm?" he asked distractedly.

"Why did you buy all of these tiny cartons of milk? It would have been cheaper to buy a gallon."

"Here it is," he said, ignoring my question.

A green cotton shirt flew through the air, and I snatched it with my left hand. I unfolded it and drew the soft fabric up against my chest. The color was pretty. Did he think about me when he bought the garment?

"My sister picked it out," he said, looking at me with an unreadable, empty expression.

I wasn't disappointed because I wasn't surprised.

Caleb wasn't here because he found me interesting or pretty. He was here to pay a debt.

Right now, I was learning a valuable lesson about the stubborn streak of an honorable man.

Chapter Seven
Caleb

I didn't know why I told Mira my sister had picked out the shirt for her. I had spent an hour at Beall's trying to figure out which shirt to get. I'd never cared about women's fashion before, but I was torn between getting something nice for her and getting something she would accept. If I thought I had an icicle's chance in hell of buying her more clothes and her actually letting me, I'd have done it and not thought twice. She had an empty closet going into a relentless winter. She had a need, and I wanted to fill it. Like with the fish I couldn't help dropping at her door every time I changed. My instincts were only getting stronger, and thinking about taking care of Mira kept my animal side under control. Eli hadn't had anyone to balance him out, no one to keep him accountable or give him a job that kept his animal focused. That's why the old man had snapped, and I was going to do everything in my power to deter that fate for myself. And right now, taking care of Mira's needs was what was keeping me sane.

As astonishing as my lie was about my sister picking out the shirt, it had given me an idea. Not a complete one, just the beginnings of a niggling at the edge of my brain that said I could do something about something. I'd have to explore it more later when Mira wasn't sitting in the cab of my truck, fiddling with the radio.

An oldies station blared out the second chorus of "Eight Days a Week," and she leaned back in the passenger's seat with a sigh. She looked small and frail, cowering on the corner of the bench seat of my truck. Even with her choice in music, she still seemed uncomfortable and trapped. Like a raccoon in a cage. It was probably me making her feel uncomfortable. People in town had started acting differently around me, too. More wary. I blamed it on the bear residing under my skin. I rolled down the windows and hoped it would help.

We parked in front of Sam Burns's office near the end of Main Street. "I'll wait out here," I told her as she escaped the truck and shut the door gingerly behind her.

Mira turned and placed her hands gently over the window opening. "Okay, I'll be right back."

I opened my mouth to tell her she didn't have to worry about being gentle with my ride. It was only a work truck, but she turned and scampered into Burns's office before I could get a word out. It wouldn't have mattered, anyway. If she wasn't comfortable with something, she wouldn't want to risk leaving any evidence she had ever been there. I didn't know how I knew that, but I did.

Two older ladies sat in rocking chairs outside of the handmade furniture shop beside the lawyer's office. I gave them a two-fingered wave out the window. "How are you doing today, ladies?"

"Caleb McCreedy. Lands alive, is that you?" Mrs. Brendel asked. She used to teach me in Sunday school when I was little.

The chair creaked rhythmically beneath her as she rocked, and the motion lulled me to relax despite my earlier tension.

"Yes ma'am, in town for some errands."

The other woman looked back to the door of Mr. Burns's office. I recognized her, too, but couldn't put a name to her face. "Is my eyesight failing or was that Mira Fletcher I just saw get out of your truck?" the woman asked.

I groaned internally. "Yes ma'am," was all I said.

"Hmph," the women said in unison.

After a moment of staring at the door Mira had disappeared into, the quieter one said, "Caleb McCreedy, you be careful with that one. You are a prominent figure in this town."

How was I supposed to respond to that? I wanted to tell her my father was the prominent member in town. I was just a member. But most of all, I wanted the tell her to advise me again after she'd had an actual conversation with Mira. Instead, I said, "Y'all have a nice day," then rolled up my window to deter any more unsolicited life advice. And so we sat, an awkward trio of semi-strangers watching the same door for the same unsuspecting girl to appear. I couldn't help but notice when the women's heads tipped together like a little pyramid of gossip as they whispered. For some reason, it really bothered me.

Maybe I was going crazy. A month and a half ago, I wouldn't have given another thought to some old ladies gossiping about Mira Fletcher. Everybody did it. So what? There wasn't much to talk about in a small town, bar the goings on of its residents, and Mira was the most interesting person to talk about. Maybe that was because people had been so creative with the stories they put out there about her over the years, or maybe because of the known truths about her sordid past that accompanied the rumors, but I was beginning to think that mostly it was because no one knew a single real thing about her. The unknown scared people. It conjured gossip. Maybe it was as simple as that for the townspeople, but it had consequences for Mira.

The door opened, and I sat up a little straighter. Whether it was because I was relieved to see her or because I was ready to drive the hell away from this awkward situation, I couldn't tell.

I reached over and swung her door open for her, but Mira stopped when she saw something on the ground. She bent over to pick it up. It was a penny someone had dropped. The thought of that penny meaning so much to anyone put a raw feeling in my gut, but instead of pocketing it, Mira flipped it over neatly and replaced it in the exact spot she had found it.

"Why did you do that?" I asked as she climbed in and shut the door.

She stared at me in confusion.

"The penny. Why'd you flip the penny?"

"Oh," she said. "It was on tails. It's bad luck to pick one up on tails, so I flipped it to heads so someone else will have good luck."

And that, I decided, wasn't all I wanted to know about Mira Fletcher.

It was, however, all I needed to know.

****

"Why didn't you tell me the favor you needed was for electric work on Crazy Mira's land?" my brother, Brian, asked. He'd been grumbling since the moment we turned onto Dark Corner Road.

"Don't call her that," I said, shutting the door to my truck a little too soundly.

"What's going on with you?" he demanded, slamming his own.

"Nothing's going on." I pulled two full plastic bags out of the bed of the truck and handed one to my sister, Sadey.

"Something's going on," Brian said.

"Just lay off, Brian. I asked for a favor and you said you would do it. If I would've known you were going to piss and moan so much, I would have just asked Drew to do it."

"Drew is a lightning rod. My work is better."

"Which is why I asked you. Plus, I didn't think you were going to rag on me so much. You're acting like Evan." Low blow, but I was pissed with the twenty questions. "Don't be that guy."

He grabbed his tools, backpack, and huge duffle bag out of the back of the truck. "No, it's cool. I feel like hiking through a haunted forest on my only day off," he said dramatically. "Except this is the part in the horror films where the sidekick," he said, pointing at himself, "disappears, only to be found nine scenes later hanging from a tree with his face eaten off."

"What is wrong with you?" Sadey asked, shaking her head.

I could see the goose bumps on her arms from where I was standing.

"Finished?" I asked.

"No, I'm not. Do you like her?" He searched my face like it would hold the answer.

"Yeah, and you would too if you actually talked to her."

"Not like that, Caleb. You know what I mean."

I growled and rubbed my hands over my face before I unhooked the small gate to Mira's property. I couldn't tell him what my real problem was, or what I'd become, but I'd be damned if I started lying to my family. I'd give him as much as I could and hope it was enough. "Look, Mira saved my life. And I don't just mean saved it. I mean she used up every last ounce of energy she had in her body to drag my carcass up to her house. She probably hadn't eaten in days. You didn't see her lying there, passed out, because of the effort she had put into getting me on her horse. Her stomach was rumbling so loud I thought it was the damned grizzly back to finish me off. She's young, scared, has no family, has been through God-knows-what and she was still cool with standing over a stranger and shooting a bear." I stopped walking and turned on Brian who was following quietly behind Sadey.

"Do you know how many hours I was out there with that grizzly? Thirteen hours, and most of that time in the pitch black. Think about that, Brian. It was playing with me. Letting me bleed out slowly like it was punishing me. If I moved to try and save myself, it swatted me down like I was nothing and went back to eating my horse. I could hear him crunching its bones, knowing that it would be me next. It would leave for hours only to come back again and again, and each time I thought *this is it. He's going to kill me now.* And a part of me was relieved by the end because it hurt so damned bad, I was ready. I owe her."

"That's not what I asked," Brian said quietly.

I puffed air out of my cheeks and started walking again. He wouldn't get an answer from me. I didn't even understand the reasons I was here.

"Why didn't you tell anyone what it was like?" Sadey asked. "You never talk about it. That stuff is poison in your mind, Caleb. You have to get it out."

Of course Sadey would think that way. She was so like my mother had been. She thought talking about problems solved problems.

"I feel like I'm talking about it all the time. It's all I ever think about, dream about. And if I have a moment of peace when I'm not thinking about it, someone is staring at my scars and reminding me all over again. Talking about it doesn't feel better. *This* doesn't feel better. The only thing that takes my mind off of everything is thinking about how to fix Mira's place up for her and pay her back for what she did."

Mira was an addictive distraction.

Brian clapped me on the back, and I winced in pain. Everything still ached.

"Sorry, man," he said. "You won't hear any more complaints from me." He grinned wickedly. "But if she cooks me for dinner you have to engrave *I told you so* on my gravestone."

I ignored him and picked up the pace. We had come to an incline and carrying all of the gear was starting to wear on my legs. I was ready to get over the hill.

"How old is she?" Sadey asked breathlessly, changing the subject.

I had never worried about bringing my sister. She was sensitive and kind and a great buffer.

"She's around your age. Just turned twenty."

"Does she know I'm coming?" Sadey sounded nervous.

I almost felt bad for going through with my plan before telling anyone. "No. I didn't want to stress her out any more than she is already."

Brian cursed softly when the house came into view. I tried to look at it from new eyes. Maybe I had just become used to its dilapidated appearance in all of my visits here, both human and bear. In all fairness to my brother, it did look like one of the old abandoned shanties off the highway outside of town. They weren't fit to house livestock, much less serve as a home for someone.

Brian and Sadey followed me up the porch steps. The front door had been propped open with an old chair and the smell of bacon and eggs wafted out, reminding my stomach that my bagel breakfast that morning hadn't been sufficient.

As I brought my hand up to the door frame to knock, I heard the soft cadence of an old record, more scratch than music, and something more. The sound of Mira's voice stopped my fist mid-knock.

"I don't know, Brady. What do you think we should do?" Mira asked in a faraway voice.

She stood over her stove, cooking breakfast and talking to her deceased uncle as if he were in the room, and the realization made my heart slink to my ankles. She wasn't right. Misfortune had wound itself into every strand of her life, and it had caught up to her. No one could survive what Mira had and come through to the other side undamaged. My siblings leaned over my shoulder to see what held me up.

"Electricity sure would make the winter more bearable up here," she continued, unaware of our presence. "Maybe you'll stick around this time, huh?"

The fine hairs on my body stood on end and made my skin feel prickled and raw. Watching madness wasn't for the weak.

"Settle down," she said. "No one's here. You always think someone is watching us."

Could old Brady Fletcher really see us from the grave? The thought made me fidgety and uncomfortable. "Mira?" I asked. "Are you okay?"

Mira jumped like a frightened jack rabbit and clutched her chest. A squeak escaped her parted lips and her eyebrows drew up in startled fear. A huge dog leaped up from its unseen position beside the stove and let out a menacing growl.

"Brady!" Mira said, recovering enough to wrap her hands through the collar at the dog's throat.

"You named your dog after your deceased uncle?" I asked, shocked and a little angry, as if I'd been tricked.

The dog was scrabbling toward the door, teeth bared and ready for a fight. Mira was losing the battle. "It's not my dog. I didn't name him. It was my uncle's harebrained idea to name him after himself."

The relief I felt was tangible. I could almost pluck it out of the air like the tight string of a guitar. Talking to one's dead relative like they were sitting at the breakfast table? Creepy. Talking to a dog like it could understand you? Not so bad.

I squatted down and offered my knuckles for the mutt to sniff. He growled again, but I lifted my lip and let out a low rumble too low for the others to hear. Brady-the-dog tucked his tail and bolted for the door, then disappeared into the woods out front.

"He doesn't like strangers," Mira said apologetically.

From the way she looked fearfully at my siblings who hovered in the doorway, she likely shared her dog's sentiments.

"Mira, this is my brother, Brian, and my little sister, Sadey," I said, introducing them.

Mira smiled shyly at Sadey and squinted at Brian. "I know you," she said. "You were outside of the clinic."

I looked at Brian questioningly.

"Mira came to visit you at the clinic," he explained. "Your girlfriend wouldn't let her through the front doors, though."

If I hadn't been turning to look at Mira for further explanation, I would have missed the fallen look on her face.

"Becca?" I guessed, and Mira nodded.

A tiny triumphant feeling ignited in my gut that I would have to think about later. I'd been wrong. Mira had come to visit me after all, the brave woman.

I set the bag I was carrying inside of the doorway and nodded for Sadey to do the same.

"How long have you been out of power up here?" Brian asked, taking on his taskmaster voice. He knelt down and opened his bag to check his equipment for the third time this morning. His thoroughness was part of what made him so good.

"We haven't had electricity since I've lived here, but we had a generator that powered what we needed. That went out about nine months ago."

Brian's head shot up, and his mouth hung open. "You haven't had any power for nine months?"

Mira's cheeks turned the most appealing shade of pink, and I couldn't take my eyes off the attractive color against the smooth porcelain of her skin.

"No, sir," she said quietly. "I thought you guys could have some breakfast before you start working. I made some eggs and bacon and biscuits."

"You didn't have to spend your groceries on us," I said.

"I wanted to. It's the only way I can repay you right now."

Sadey cut in. She understood proud people because she had been raised with them. "Smells good, Mira. Do you need any help?"

Mira looked relieved and let out a little puff of a sigh. "Maybe you could set the table?"

The girls got to work and, for lack of something to do, I took the two plastic bags Sadey had brought into Mira's room. I placed them by the door and looked around. She had made her bed, and the green shirt I'd bought her was draped over a wooden chair in the corner of her room as if she were trying to keep the wrinkles from it.

The sight made me smile, and the stretch of my lips felt good. It had been a long time since I had allowed a grin on my face.

Chapter Eight
Mira

Breakfast had been one part relief and two parts terrifying. Brian and Caleb had remained silent for the bulk of it, but Sadey had kept up a running commentary that included me answering questions about myself. There were only so many ways to avoid speaking on the subject, which had made me most uncomfortable. She didn't seem to be doing it out of spite, though. On the contrary, she seemed as if she was actually interested.

Brian had stalled on taking the first bite for so long that Caleb had glared at him until he was halfway through and had complimented my cooking. It made me feel uncomfortable for him, so I ate at warp speed to have an excuse to leave the table. When I had stood to rinse my dishes, the atmosphere in the room seemed to relax and Caleb bantered easily with Sadey. I smiled over my dishes at their ease with each other and wished I'd had a sibling growing up. If, for nothing else, just to pacify the ache of loneliness that seemed to hover around this place like a storm cloud.

The legs of the dining chair scuttled across the wooden floor as Caleb pulled out from his place at the table. I turned my head slightly to watch him approach. He hadn't shaved this morning, and his chin sported dark blond stubble, which only made me want to touch it just to see what his casual face felt like. I wouldn't dare, but the urge was still present. My stomach clenched as he approached with an easy smile over something Sadey had said to him. His eyes looked off to the left as if he were thinking on the conversation, but I could still see their brilliant cerulean color. Whatever animal instincts I'd dredged up yesterday, his family didn't have the same effect on his inner bear. He placed his dishes in the sink, and in a gesture so comfortable and casual and unexpected, he placed his hand on my hip to let me know he needed me to scoot over so he could get to the trashcan beneath the sink. My breath caught at his touch, and I lifted my startled gaze to him. His wide eyes met mine and held me.

"I'm sorry," he breathed.

He was so close to me that I could feel the tickle of his breath and the power that rolled off his skin, as if it was a natural part of him. I pulled away first because I would explode if I stayed captured in his gaze another moment. The absence of his hand over the thin material of my worn tank top was a dull ache. The skin there felt cold, as if it was missing something vital it didn't know it had needed. He threw his used napkin into the small trashcan and headed back to the table. When I could draw a steady breath again, I began rinsing his dishes.

"What?" he asked ruefully, and I turned to see Brian and Sadey staring at him like their brother had just grown antlers. "Come on, Brian, let's get this done," Caleb clipped as his brother rose from the table. "Sadey, I'm going to help him out today. You okay to stay here for a while?"

I saw nervousness in Sadey's wide eyes, but above that there was a brave determination. I liked her more for it.

"I'll stay here with Mira. We have girlie stuff to take care of."

That sounded downright terrifying, but no eight words had ever scared off two men faster, and I soon found myself completely alone with Sadey McCreedy, youngest heir to the McCreedy fortune. I was intimidated into silence. Hell, I was surprised I wasn't in a stress coma yet, but she took charge and led me into my room.

"I have something I want to show you, but I don't want you to get upset. Caleb told me a little bit about you," Sadey explained. She looked at the hurt on my face and specified. "All good stuff, I swear. But he said you wouldn't accept clothes. I'm going to beg you to reconsider. Woman to woman."

I had already started shaking my head. I was nobody's charity case, and it didn't sit well with me that he'd been telling people I needed clothing.

She turned away from my negative answer and rifled through one of the bags against the wall nearest the empty dresser.

"Don't say no until you see this," she said through a smile as she pulled out a white summer dress with a light pink satin ribbon around the waist. The straps were thick, made to fan the tips of feminine collar bones.

I bit my lip. It really was the most beautiful dress I'd ever seen in person. It seemed Sadey could feel my resolve falter because she pounced.

"I swear," she whispered earnestly. "I'll never, ever tell anyone I gave you these."

"Where'd you get them?" I asked, standing on tiptoes and stretching my neck to peer into the opened bag.

"They were mine. I already had them bagged up to take into the city. I wanted to donate them, but then Caleb said he thought you were about the same size as me." Sadey pulled shirts, pants, jeans, shorts, dresses, and shoes out one by one. "If you don't like any of them, we'll re-bag them and donate the cast offs."

My eyes kept traveling back to the white sundress.

Sadey grinned brightly. "Try it on."

And try it on I did. Except I didn't stop with the sundress. I tried on every single piece of clothing Sadey had brought. A lot of the colors were made for Sadey's skin tone. She had blond hair like Caleb and fair skin, and some of the pastel colors that looked so amazing against her complexion made me look like I had jaundice, but who was I to be choosey? In the end, I only tossed two shirts that were much too short back into the bag.

My emotions were everywhere. As if I had just gone on the longest shopping trip in creation, I was exhausted. On the other hand, I had actually had fun trying on the beautiful clothes, knowing that tomorrow morning I would wake up and have a choice.

I laughed, the noise sounding foreign. I plopped on top of the pile of clothes on my bed and pretended I was swimming. Sadey had taken up the chair beside my bed and laughed as she folded up three pair of jeans that were way too loose on me but would be helpful during the cold winter.

"Mira, do you want me to cut your hair?" she asked suddenly, as if she were saying it before she lost the nerve to do so.

I hadn't had my hair cut in a really long time. Not from lack of wanting, but from lack of resources.

"Do you know how?" I asked hopefully.

"I'm going to beauty school after I graduate. I cut a lot of my friends' hair already. I can do yours, too, but only if you want me to."

I sat up and looked at my unruly tresses in the rusted mirror above my dresser. True, my dark locks were overwhelming, but what would I hide my face with? Then another thought occurred, one that was frightening for what it could mean to me and my stupidly hopeful heart. Would Caleb like it?

"How would you cut it?" I asked.

"Well, you can choose, but if it were me, I'd keep it long."

A wave of relief washed over me that she got it.

She continued. "You have a really pretty natural wave, and if we cut some of the weight off and layer it up, your curls would be looser and more manageable. It would look really cute in a ponytail, too, if you ever felt like putting it up."

That actually sounded kind of perfect. "Okay," I said. "When do we start?"

The cool day told of autumn approaching, but we decided to cut my hair outside on the front porch. Sadey had washed my hair in the bathroom sink, and now I leaned comfortably into an old chair with my feet crossed at the ankle over the creaking front porch railing. The pull and play of my hair was relaxing, and I couldn't help but be lulled into a state of half-consciousness. Beautiful moments were rare in this life, and I was determined to enjoy this one thoroughly.

"Is Becca really Caleb's girlfriend?" I asked drowsily.

Sadey remained silent, and I regretted having ruined the moment. I don't know why I'd felt comfortable enough to say anything at all, much less an embarrassingly transparent question like that one.

"There," she said, snipping the scissors neatly one last time. She placed the scissors and comb precariously on the splintered railing and took a seat on the front steps. She didn't answer my question until her back was settled against a large wooden pillar. With a faraway look into the woods, she said, "I don't know that Caleb's ever had a girlfriend."

I rested my head against the back of the chair and waited.

"Becca has liked him for a long time. I mean *really* liked him. But Caleb hasn't ever formed an attachment to a girl. He took her out a few times last year but moved on and seemed unaffected." She turned her soft green gaze to me. "I haven't ever quite figured him out. I'll tell you two things, and maybe I'm in the wrong for doing so, but I'll give my two cents anyway. First, I hope that someday I have a man look at me the way Caleb looked at you in the kitchen this morning. But," she warned, "Caleb's different. You have to be careful with that one, Mira. I love my brother, but he isn't like other people. He doesn't need companionship like the rest of us. He is a good man and a hard worker, but I haven't actually seen him really let anyone in. Ever."

He didn't sound so different to me. He sounded *like* me. I understood the loneliness that came along with pushing others away.

"Also, Becca is a bunion. I'm glad she isn't my sister-in-law," Sadey said through a mischievous grin.

The idea of Caleb and marriage startled me. "How old is he?" I asked, suddenly feeling very young.

"Twenty-three goin' on thirty-five. If any of us has a chance of taking over Dad's business, it's him. He has the head and the work ethic for it."

It was approaching lunchtime, and I was searching for something to do with Sadey to keep her from getting bored. I guessed the electrical work would take all day. "You want to take lunch out to the boys?" I asked.

"Sounds good. How will we find them though? Your place is pretty big."

"I have a couple of horses out back. Do you ride?"

She bit her lip. "I have before, but I wasn't very good at it. Horses kind of scare me." Her admission gave her brownie points in my book.

"You don't have to be afraid of these horses. They are older than dirt and sweeter than honey."

"Let's do it," she said with determination. "I could use an adventure. Wait. What about the bears up here?"

I waved my hand nonchalantly. Her brother was the only bear around here, and I doubted he was any danger to her right now. "Nah, you don't have to worry about them. The one that got Caleb is dead, and they are pretty territorial. Plus they aren't native to Texas. There won't be any more grizzlies around these parts." I hoped it was true. "I'll bring a rifle if it'll make you feel better, though."

"Okay," Sadey said. Her green eyes held an attractive combination of uncertainty and excitement.

It was still early in the day so we took our time making sandwiches and saddling the horses. I had Sadey brush out Blue before she attempted the blanket and saddle. The extra time primping him seemed to make her feel more comfortable. Probably because he stood there like a brick with his back hoof propped up and resting, like he would either fall asleep or die on her at any moment. It was hard to be intimidated by a horse that acted as if it had taken a dose of moose tranquilizers instead of alfalfa cubes for breakfast.

Bobby was more of an ornery old cuss, but I liked that about him. Every time he bit at me or tried to rub me off on a tree, I marveled at the effort he put into ridding himself of riders. His habits hadn't changed with old age, and I appreciated his stubbornness. I liked to think that, like my old rusty truck, no one could start him but me.

The ride was comfortable and the conversation easy, but I couldn't take credit for that. Sadey could probably charm a tree into discussion. She told me about school, about her friends, and what she did for fun. She talked about some of the town's upcoming social events. She had a knack for telling stories, and they kept me enraptured. That and the lives of the town's residents were an enigma that I had never managed to solve, but still wanted to. Hearing tales of the town from someone who inhabited the sweet candy center of it made me like the people there. Almost.

"I see them," Sadey said, pointing excitedly through the woods to the front line of my property. She sat up proudly and grinned.

"Good eye, Sadey," I said as I squinted to catch the movement she had seen.

The boys were huddled near a wooden post that held up power lines off Dark Corner Road. Caleb saw us first, and his eyes landed on my new shorter hair. I couldn't read his expression, and I hadn't looked at it in the mirror so I grew self-conscious. Back went my hair into a ponytail as fast as my nimble fingers could manage. I wished I could hide, but we had already been spotted, and Sadey was waving wildly.

"We brought lunch," she sang as our horses picked their way around mesquite brush and close enough for them to hear.

"Good," Brian grumbled over his shoulder. "Saves us a hike back up to the house."

As he approached Bobby and Blue, Caleb's boot prints kicked up little clouds of dry sand. He slipped his fingers into their halters and held them while Sadey and I dismounted. Bobby flattened his ears and curled his lips back to nip at Caleb, but he jerked the horse's head down with a stout yank on the reins, and Bobby was wise enough not to try it again. I did my best to hide my smile. I couldn't help myself. Bobby's naughty antics had always entertained me.

"Don't encourage him," Caleb chastised me, but the corners of his lips had turned up slightly, and I waited for a remorse that didn't come.

After the horses were tied, Sadey and I unpacked the saddle bags and laid out an old blanket. The blanket had belonged to my grandfather and was made of a patchwork of old jeans and shirts he and his brothers had outworn. If it was anything at all, it was unique.

"This should take us a few more hours, but it won't be longer than that," Brian said around a bite of turkey sandwich. "Looks like someone tried to patch you in before me. I don't think they knew what they were doing, but they did some of the work for us. Was it your uncle?"

I shrugged. I had stopped trying to guess at Uncle Brady's actions after the first week of living with the man. I finished chewing and swallowed an enormous bite to find my three lunch mates all looking at me, waiting for an answer. Human conversation would probably never come easy for me.

"Oh. I'm not sure. I never saw him messing with any of it, but then again I didn't spend a lot of time with him during the day. He liked to stay away from the house. Or away from me."

I had answered honestly, but my response seemed to make them uncomfortable. I didn't offer any more answers for the remainder of our short lunch. It had never been my intention to make them squirm. I wished they would just learn their lesson and stop asking questions. There were no happy or witty stories in my repertoire like Sadey had. I couldn't, for the life of me, even remember a happy memory other than the day I spent with Caleb after the attack, and that had been traumatizing and bloody.

It was hard leaving Caleb to his work. I worked slowly to pack up our trash and blanket, and my gaze slid to study his silhouette as he dusted off his pants and pulled an old baseball cap over his blond hair. Brian watched me, and the unsolicited attention made it easier to focus on getting Sadey back into the saddle.

"I still can't believe you got Sadey on a horse," Caleb said in his deep southern drawl, a smile in his voice. I wanted to look to see if the smile I heard was really on his face, but I looked at the ground instead.

"Ah, it wasn't me. She's a natural," I said.

Sadey positively glowed under the compliment. "See you boys back at the house," she said as she pulled Blue around and away from her brothers.

I waved at Caleb and turned before he could respond.

One of the foster families I had stayed with had ignored me. No matter what I did or said, there was absolutely no response from the people I'd been struggling to connect with. There were other children in the house. Children more in my foster parents' favor who would elicit compliments and, in turn, reprimands from them. I would have given my left arm to be reprimanded. At least if they'd made the effort to correct my behavior, it would have meant they cared and I wasn't just a means to a small monthly check for them.

Being ignored was the loneliest feeling on the planet. By the time I had come to stay with Uncle Brady, I had been trained to ignore the hurt. Or to accept it. All of my training had flown out the window when Caleb McCreedy entered my life, and the need for his approval left me feeling unbalanced.

I lay awake for a long time that night. Caleb would finish paying whatever debt he thought he had accrued, and I would never see him again except for accidental meetings on my rare trips into town. How would I ever be able to go back to the loneliness of my previous life? I was weak for letting a man affect me so, and I became determined to be colder.

I could turn my heart off.

I had done it a hundred times before.

Chapter Nine
Mira

I stared at the tiny cartons of milk that lined the refrigerator. I'd seen the small cartons in the miniature fridge at Jake's and thought how neat it would be to drink out of one, but it seemed inefficient and wasteful. The empty carton was a small weight in my hand, and I counted fourteen left. I had no guess why Caleb had bought these instead of a gallon of milk. Maybe he didn't have a concept of saving money or of being frugal. The purchase seemed at odds with the man I had an occasional clipped conversation with. Honestly, his disregard for money bothered me.

I jumped as a loud car horn blasted from right outside the front door. The sound echoed through the house and settled into my bones.

I threw open the front door. "What are you doing?" I asked Caleb, who was sitting in his truck on the front lawn.

"I widened the gate. Go get ready. We're heading into town."

"Why?" I asked as my heart skittered.

"Because we need to find you a way to earn a living, and it's not going to get done from here."

He sounded irritated, but maybe it was just because he wasn't a morning person. I'd take that over annoyance directed at me any day of the week.

"Do you want breakfast?" I asked.

"You're stalling," he accused. "We'll grab something in town."

Breakfast in town sounded absolutely terrifying. Not even a little part of me wanted anything to do with such an excursion.

I turned to retreat back into the house. Maybe he would leave if I took long enough.

"Wear the green shirt," he called out from the open window of his truck.

Or maybe he wouldn't leave.

"What did I do?" I mumbled under my breath as I headed for the bathroom.

One green shirt, a pair of stretch jeans that didn't look half bad, and a pair of Sadey's black flats later and I was shutting the door behind me. The shoes were a little big but if I shuffled, they stayed put.

"You look…" Caleb started. He cleared his throat. "You ready?"

"As I'll ever be," I murmured.

"Good. Good attitude to have," he said as he edged his truck down a path he had apparently just bulldozed with the front end of his truck.

"As I'll ever be means no," I said testily. "Why are you doing this to me?" I didn't mean to sound whiney, but I really didn't want to leave the comfort of my own home today. People didn't insult me and throw things at me here.

Caleb took off the old gray baseball cap he was wearing and scratched his head. The movement seemed to be more about agitation and less about an itch. "Mira, I'm not doing anything to upset you. Not on purpose. It's important that the people in town get used to seeing you and being around you and eating next to you. The more you alienate yourself out here, the less they will be able to relate to you."

"Well, maybe I like the way things are." Even I could hear the false note in my voice.

"You like it when people are mean to you when you come into town?" he asked.

I didn't answer. Instead, I rested my head on the window and did my best to ignore him—if anyone could really ignore Caleb McCreedy in such close quarters.

"No? That's what I thought. They're in the wrong, Mira. I'm not defending them, but if anyone is going to make it right, it's got to be you. You have to be the bigger person on this one."

"But I'm a very tiny person," I said, dragging my beseeching gaze over to him.

He looked at me in confusion, and then back to the road. Back at me, then back at the road again. I helped him out with a tiny smile, and he surprised me with a laugh, short and loud.

In a softer tone, he said, "I know you can do this. It's just going to take some time." He seemed to relax, and he hooked his arm over back of the bench seat between us.

I held my breath. If I exhaled it would shake—I knew it would. His arm wasn't around me, but just a few seconds ago, I'd been sitting in front of where his hand was resting. As it were, his fingertips could almost touch the tip of my collarbone had he the mind to do so.

He didn't. The trip commenced with his arm arched in an almost-touch, and me breathing as lightly as I could without fainting cold against the window.

When Caleb pulled the truck into a parking spot in front of Rooney's Bar, I raised my eyebrows and nodded. Classy.

"They serve breakfast," he explained. "Jake's serves a mean lunch, but nobody can beat Rooney's pancakes."

The mention of the delectable, butter-soaked, golden edibles brought an embarrassingly loud grumble from my stomach. He gave me an I-told-you-so look and shut the truck door behind him. I wanted to kick him.

I could refuse to get out of the truck. I turned the thought over in my mind, but one look at him hopping off the curb to open my door for me stomped out that notion. I had no doubt he would drag me bodily from this vehicle. That or he would be disappointed in me, which would be even worse.

Caleb reached for the door, and my naughty little finger pushed down on the lock button just as he pulled the handle. His startled face was enough to better my mood, and I grinned at him through the window before pushing the unlock button. He tried to look irritated but mostly he looked amused. I slid out of the truck, and Caleb shut the door behind me so firmly that my hands went over my ears before I could stop them. Why did he have to be so rough with everything? It was like the built up power he possessed in his body leaked out at random times throughout the day. Caleb wasn't a gentle or apologetic creature. He was a man born of raw masculinity and strength. I wondered how much of that had been from before the attack and how much was from the animal inside of him now.

"Come on," he said, pressing his hand lightly against the small of my back to get my legs moving.

I pulled my hands away from my ears and allowed him to lead me to the door of Rooney's. What other choice did I have? My legs were threatening to collapse under his touch.

When I tried to scuttle into the booth in the back corner, Caleb switched directions and led me to a table at the very center of the busy eatery. I wanted to curse, but I kept my colorful words to myself.

Breakfast was just as horrifyingly awkward as I imagined it would be. Caleb acted as if he didn't notice everyone staring at us. I, however, felt the weight of the unwanted attention with every bite I took. I wished I could just enjoy the food. I was a decent cook, but there was just something about someone else cooking for you that made it taste better. That, and I hadn't had pancakes in years. And eating syrup was downright orgasmic.

Caleb lacked the ease with which his sister conversed, but I was impressed with the effort. He waited for me to order my meal before he started talking. Mostly he talked about his plans for my house, which were interesting, but not quite as much as the way his mouth moved when he talked. I was scattered and unfocused and his every movement seemed to demand my attention. Everyone's whispered mumblings about the unlikely event of one Caleb McCreedy taking one Crazy Mira Fletcher to breakfast like we were long time pals was borderline overwhelming to my sensitive ears. I imagined the town collectively crapping a sea urchin at what transpired in Rooney's Bar this morning.

I pushed my last two pancakes around my plate. I'd been starving when we walked through the door and smelled the home cooking, but sitting under a magnifying glass the entire meal as everyone in Rooney's leaned closer to hear our conversation made me lose my appetite. Caleb frowned at my unfinished meal.

"Excuse me, Sarah?" he asked our waitress as she bustled by our table. "Could we get a to-go box? And the check whenever you have a minute."

"Sure," she said sweetly. Sarah slid a glance in my direction and then back to Caleb before she leaned closer to him and lowered her voice. "Anything for a McCreedy," she said through a flirty smile that boasted much too much dark lipstick.

When she came back with a to-go box and the check, I looked curiously across the table at the tiny, white piece of paper to see how much a breakfast for two cost. Caleb pulled out a wadded up ten and a five from his pocket and put them under a plastic cylinder that held the sugar. He crumpled up the receipt, but not before I saw the waitress's phone number written across the top of it.

I stared at him as he downed the rest of his coffee. How many times had girls given their numbers to him in hopes that he would call? From the way he flippantly threw it in the trashcan on his way out, it probably happened regularly.

He took a toothpick from a small plastic container on the front counter and offered it to me. I declined politely and headed for the door as he exchanged small talk with an older gentleman behind the bar.

"What do you think you are doing?" a woman asked as I stepped outside.

Automatically, I sidestepped the flurry of motion I saw coming in fast from my right. Becca.

"What are you doing with Caleb? Are you stupid, or is it unclear to you that we are a thing?" she asked. "Why on earth would he be eating breakfast, for the entire town to see, with a freak like you?"

There really was no need to try and keep up my end of the conversation. A response from me seemed completely unnecessary.

Becca lowered her voice and laughed. "I bet he is trying to make me jealous." She turned a death glare on me. "Won't work, though. I'd never be jealous of Crazy Mira."

Caleb cleared his throat from behind me. Annoyance soaked his tone when he asked, "Everything okay here, ladies?"

"What are you doing?" Becca whisper-screamed. "Did you even think about how embarrassing this would be for me? I had to find out about this"—Becca waved her hand frantically in my direction—"from Nora Leadby, and she heard it from, like, thirty other people!"

"Believe it or not," Caleb said, putting his hand on my hip to push me toward the truck, "I didn't think about you when I asked Mira to breakfast. You and I aren't together, Becca. We never really were, so I'd appreciate it if you left her alone."

Caleb took his sweet time tucking me into the truck and sauntering around the front, looking as if he didn't at all notice everyone gathered outside of Rooney's staring blatantly. He gave the crowd a friendly wave and a, "Y'all have a good day," and then we were off to the butcher shop so I could apply for a job. Again.

Caleb, after seeing my apparent lack of fear when it came to bloodier situations, had decided a job in the back at Don's Butcher Shop would be the perfect one for me. I didn't really care, nor was I picky. I'd do anything shy of standing on a street corner with my boobs out to earn some money if it meant I'd reclaim my independence.

A more disappointed look I had never seen on anyone's face than on Butcher Don's when I walked through the door to his shop.

"What can I do you for, Miss Fletcher?" he drawled, wiping his hands on his apron. It was clear as water he hoped I was ordering a pound of beefsteak.

I clenched my hands together to steady them as I approached the counter. "Your sign still says you're hiring. I think I would fit what you need. I process my own game and am comfortable with a knife. Would you mind if I filled out an application?"

I could see the answer written all over his face before he even opened his mouth to speak. "Mira, I just don't have a position open for someone like you."

I left the butcher shop about thirty seconds later, having received almost, word for word, the same rejection I had obtained two months ago.

Caleb sat in the truck with the stereo blaring. His arm dangled comfortably out of the window, and he raised it in a *what the hell* gesture when I hurried across the sidewalk to hop into the cab.

"What happened? You weren't even in there a minute," he said.

I shrugged miserably. "Mr. Don said the same thing he said last time."

Caleb growled. It was the only word I had for the angry noise that burst from his throat. "Come on," he ordered before I even had the chance to warm my fingers by the heater.

"Caleb, it's fine—"

"No, it's not, Mira. It's fucked up," he said, heading for my side of the truck.

I slithered out of the cab before he could reach the door. "Okay," I muttered, shutting the door gently behind me. That creaking metal door didn't even know I had just saved it from the slamming of its life.

"Caleb," Don greeted with a smile. His face fell when he realized I was hiding behind him.

"Don Forbes, you have a sign up on the door that says you're hiring, and you won't even let her fill out a damned application for it?" Caleb asked. The walls seemed to move inward with the volume of his voice. "She has a high school diploma, which is more than I can say for the last dipshit who worked here. She knows her way around an animal, and she's strong enough to handle what you need her to. What's the hold up?"

"Caleb," the portly man behind the counter said low. "It ain't that I don't want to help her out. It's just I'm barely making it right now. I can't handle a dip in business, or I'll lose it. She," he said jabbing a finger in my direction, "will scare off all of my business, even if she doesn't mean to. I can't help you. I have a family to take care of."

Caleb swung his gaze to me, and I grabbed his forearm when I noticed the gold in his eyes. "It's okay."

"It's not," he argued, tilting his head.

He began to turn away from me, but I flung my arms around his shoulders and held him close. "Your eyes," I breathed. "We need to go."

He rubbed the side of my face, his short stubble rasping against my cheek. "Okay." His grip tightened on my waist, and my legs went numb. I wanted to stay like this forever, holding him. It had been an impulsive thing to do, but he'd reacted in the most unexpected way. Like he was enjoying my touch.

Caleb inhaled a long breath and stepped around me and through the front door, leaving me to try and look like I hadn't just had the most life-altering moment of my entire existence.

"Sorry, Mr. Don," I murmured, then spun for the door.

"This ain't right," Caleb fumed from the driver's side of his truck. His deep southern drawl came out more when he was angry. He wasn't even trying to keep his eyes human-looking right now, and I tossed up a little thank-you that the windows of Caleb's truck were heavily tinted.

"It's not right, but he has a point," I said. "I would hurt business for anyone in town."

I didn't know why I was defending any of them from the wrath of a McCreedy. They had never lifted a finger for me, unless it was to throw stuff.

Caleb threw the truck into reverse, and we headed back up Main Street. "There isn't any real point in trying to find you a job right now. The answer will be the same with everyone."

I curled my knees to my chin and leaned up against the door. Caleb was quiet on the way back to my house, but it was the kind of silence that had weight. I looked at him exactly two times to blazing eyes and no response. He was completely lost in thought, enough to miss the turnoff for Dark Corner.

Was he disappointed with me? Had he realized I was a lost cause and that he was wasting his time trying to help me carve out a life in this town?

I kept my questions to myself for fear that he would confirm my racing suspicions. My rejection cup was full for the day.

Some time alone at the house would do wonders for recovery after this morning. I didn't think he would work today. In fact, he would likely never come back to the house again. The change had been nice, but it was time for me to prepare for winter as I always did. It was time for me to recede into my woods—to become a part of them again.

Town wasn't for me. Town would never be for me.

He didn't say a word as his truck crept up the incline of the newly made dirt road to my house. As I shut the door behind me, he surprised me and leaned over to open the window.

"My family has dinner together every Sunday night at six o'clock," he said.

I waited for the punch line.

"I'll pick you up around five-thirty."

My mouth was only able to form a *wa* sound before he pulled the truck around and headed back toward the gate. He didn't look in his rearview mirror as he disappeared. I knew because I watched for him to. I waited for him to turn around and tell me he was just kidding, but as he was swallowed up by my woods, he gave no such satisfaction.

In one day's time, I would be expected to share dinner in the McCreedy den. Most of the people in town would have sold their best boots for such an unlikely invitation, and here I was in full-blown panic mode and cursing under my breath at Caleb's mile-wide stubborn streak.

I was starting to think he was trying to kill me. Clearly, Caleb's plan was to maim me slowly with food and social engagements.

Chapter Ten
Caleb

Mira was what happened to Neverland when all the lost boys had gone but one. She clung to her ever-changing, never-changing woods because it was all she knew.

For the first time in my entire life, I wished my name meant more. She'd come out of the butcher shop with that disappointed and wholly unsurprised look on her face, and I had wished I could fix it with a single word. Not for the good of the town or even for the good of Mira, but for the good of me.

She would need a letter of recommendation from someone who meant more than I did to the town. She would need to be on my father's good side, a tiny bird under his outstretched wing if she was to have a chance at getting a job.

Before, I had hated the difference in the way people had treated the McCreedys. But right now, in this moment, I wished I could use the name for more.

****

Mira

Hope was a hummingbird. Tiny in size and fragile by nature. Beautiful.

Flitting around a garden in search of an early morning drink, but my garden hadn't had roses in years and hummingbirds hadn't existed. A tiny weed had poked through the cracked and dry earth, and ever so slowly it had grown into a flower. And the hummingbirds had returned.

That's what Caleb had done for me. I was beginning to hope for more from this life, and as scary as that was, it was also exciting.

Not on Sunday, though. Sunday, my hope was the lack of noise around the house when I awoke late in the morning meant Caleb had given up and I wouldn't, in fact, be subjected to embarrassing myself in front of his father at dinner tonight.

Sadey showed up at four o'clock in the afternoon to flick my hummingbird right out of my garden.

"I thought I would come by and help you get ready," she said.

"He's still going through with this?" I couldn't hide my disappointment if I tried.

Sadey laughed like I'd been joking. "Afraid so. He already told my dad you were coming. No turning back now."

I showered and Sadey used a set of terrifying looking instruments to heat my hair into submission. I was pleasantly surprised at the effect when I looked at it in my old bedroom mirror. Instead of organized chaos around my face, it was shaped by soft and elongated waves of dark tresses that tickled my back and collar bones. She had insisted I wear the white sundress I loved so much and pinned the front of my hair to the side. She put makeup on my skin, not much, mind you, but enough to show there was effort made. My gray eyes looked even lighter in contrast with my dark hair and mascara, and my full lips held an attractive hue of deep glossy pink.

It became abundantly clear that Sadey McCreedy was a miracle worker.

"Thank you," I whispered, turning again to look at the unfamiliar girl looking back at me through the mirror.

Sadey smiled into the reflection. "Of course. You don't have to worry about tonight, you know. I'll be there, and Caleb will be there. Brian will be there, too. You'll already know half the people at the table."

"It's not you guys I'm worried about. It's your dad."

Sadey shrugged. "He's not so bad. He'll be honest about what he is thinking, but his thoughts are never cruel. To me, he is a big teddy bear."

"That's because you're his daughter, though. I am a thorn in his town."

"You'll be fine. I promise. I'd better go before Caleb shows up to pick you up. He has been in the worst mood lately."

I helped her gather all of her beauty supplies into a bright pink tote bag and followed her to the front door.

"I'll see you in a little while," she said. She turned and grabbed my hand. "Do you want me to sit beside you at the dinner table?"

"Please," I said, more grateful for her thoughtfulness than I could ever express. The idea that Sadey would be there as a buffer did actually make me feel a lot better.

Caleb arrived just half an hour later. He pulled his Ford to a halt in my front yard and I rushed out the door before he could blast the horn. He was already getting out of the truck and didn't see me until he was at the stairs of my front porch.

"Hey," I said shyly.

He glanced up at me, and his look of deep thoughtfulness turned to one of surprise. Shock, really. "Wow," he said softly.

His hand lifted slowly as he took in my dress and, not knowing what he intended, I placed my hand in his and used him to help me down the stairs. He recovered quite nicely…though he was probably just throwing his hands up in shock that I had used a brush on my hair. He opened the door to his truck and waited for me to climb in before he shut it and leaned against the open window.

His eyes were earnest and clear and his face so close to mine. "Mira, you look beautiful."

Heat crept into my cheeks and traveled to the very tips of my ears. He was waiting for me to respond, but all I could do was look into his impossibly blue eyes and fight the urge to move a strand of blond hair, which had lifted gently in the breeze, behind his ear with the tip of my finger.

When it became apparent I had frozen lamely into place and wouldn't offer a response other than the dumb smile that inched embarrassingly across my lips, he pushed off the door and strode to the driver's side. I cast my eyes heavenward and puffed air out of my cheeks in frustration.

When he climbed in, I cleared my throat. "Sadey came over to help me get ready. She did all of this."

"She did?" he asked, his golden brows winging up. He turned the engine over and it roared to life.

"Your sister is really nice," I said over the noise.

"Yeah," he agreed. "She's the best of us."

I smiled because she had said the same about him.

It was cool outside but not enough to run the heat. Caleb seemed to prefer to drive with his windows down no matter the weather. Did he feel as trapped as me in small spaces? Perhaps that was the new animal inside of him. As we crawled slowly down the rough road toward the front gate, I held my hair at the nape of my neck to keep it from whipping in the breeze and losing its curl. He noticed the movement and pulled to a stop.

"You can roll the window up if you're worried about your hair," he offered.

I hesitated. I didn't want him to think I was a girl who cared about such things. Because I wasn't. But I did want to look presentable for Mr. McCreedy.

Caleb seemed to realize my dilemma. "Best you do it so Sadey doesn't lynch me for ruining all of her hard work."

I tried to roll up the window but the lever was stuck.

"Here, let me," he said, leaning over my lap and jerking the lever a couple of times before it wised up and moved under his will.

I breathed as lightly as I could. I looked down at the musculature in his arm, easily visible under his thin, gray, cotton shirt and the strain against the window lever. His body was so close to mine, I could feel the heat, and my stomach clenched inwardly. The tops of my breasts fought for air and space against the bust of the dress, and when he straightened up, he froze in place and seemed to notice them, too.

His eyes lifted to mine, and I could see tiny flecks of green in them. I wondered if anyone else had seen those tiny specks of unexpected color but me. A piece of me wished I was the only one.

"You're beautiful, too," I whispered before I could stop myself.

The sides of his mouth turned up in the barest of smiles, and his eyes fell to my lips. He rested his hand on the other side of my leg, fingers curling against the fabric of my dress like he needed me closer. Then he leaned in and kissed me lightly on the neck.

A helpless sound came from my throat, and my body turned boneless as my eyes rolled back in my head.

"I can smell how aroused you are," Caleb murmured against the tripping pulse under my ear.

My breath came in a pant as he slid his hand up my leg and under the billowy material of my dress. I clenched his shirt in my fists and pulled him closer.

A deep chuckle reverberated against my collarbone. "Is this what you want, Mira?"

Fooling around in the cab of a truck with the man I felt more connected with than any other person on the planet? "Hell yes," I breathed.

I squeaked in shock as Caleb pulled the lever under the seat and rocketed the bench backward. In one swift motion, he pulled me over his lap and ran his hands up my legs, rucking my dress up to my hips. We were definitely going to be late to dinner, but I couldn't find it in me to care right now.

I fumbled to unbutton his shirt, but he grabbed my hand and lifted somber eyes to mine. "No."

A little hurt bloomed inside of me. "Why not? Is it the scars?"

He nodded once.

"Okay." I pulled my hand from his grasp and re-buttoned the one I'd managed to undo. I knew all about hiding scars. Patience, I could do.

Instead, I moved my fingers to the snap on his jeans and arched my eyebrow in question.

This time, a slow smile spread across his lips, and he nodded. The pop of his button was loud in the quiet of the cab.

He lifted my panties under my dress and slid his hand against my sex just as I unsheathed his erection. I bucked against his hand instinctively as he slid a long finger inside of me.

"God, you're already so wet," he murmured. He sounded almost…proud. Reaching around me with his other hand, he pulled me closer and rested his hand on my tailbone as I rocked against him. I hadn't a clue what to do right now, but as pressure built inside of me, I felt the urge to do something. Shimmying his pants down lower, I brushed my fingertip up the length of his shaft. It was so hard already, like stone, and it twitched under my touch. A soft rumble sounded from Caleb, and he relaxed into the seat. I brushed him with two fingers, his jaw clenched, and his hips rocked forward. When he opened his eyes, they were bright, with the barest hint of gold around the edges. The rattling in his throat grew louder when I wrapped my hand around his base and stroked up the length of him.

"Are you purring?" I whispered, pride surging through me. I was causing that sound.

Something changed in the way he was touching me. He adjusted the angle of his hand and pressed against a sensitive spot that had me arching against him.

"Bears don't purr. No more questions," he said in a soft, gravelly voice. "I just want you to tell me what you like."

"This."

"Yeah?"

"And touching you."

"Good," he said, rocking his hips in rhythm with mine. He pulled me even closer and pushed my panties farther to the side.

"I like being this close to you," I said. Slipping my free arm around his shoulder, I rested my forehead against his as I stroked him faster to keep up with the pace he was setting.

He cupped my sex and drove his finger deeper inside of me and I gasped at the pleasure and pain. It ached a little, but not enough to diminish how good he felt inside of me.

He pulled me against him until I could feel his shaft against my thigh. We were so close I could imagine what he would feel like to fill me, not just with his finger. He seemed to be losing control, too, because his hips jerked erratically against me, and he lowered his forehead to my chest, as if he was trying to shield the fiery color in his eyes. A growl rippled through him as I pulled another stroke of his shaft, and then another. I wished my dress wasn't in the way so I could see our skin so close.

Pressure, pressure, pressure and, "Oh!" Something was going to happen. I couldn't go on feeling this good forever. "I'm going to…Caleb!" I cried out as my body shuddered and pulsed around his finger.

He gritted his teeth and jets of wet warmth shot against my leg.

When he stilled, breath erratic as he pulled his finger out of me, I couldn't help the exhausted grin that took my face. I was different now. *We* were different, my bear man and I.

"Mira," he whispered, my name almost reverent on his lips. He cupped my face, and his beautiful, inhuman gaze dipped to my lips.

I held my breath as my heart hammered against my ribcage.

He was going to kiss me.

****

Caleb

Mira's eyes drifted closed, her dark lashes brushing her cheeks. Her lips looked so damned delicious I could barely think of anything but tasting them. How could I be thinking about kissing her like this? Like I was claiming her? She was this exotic wounded bird, and I was a freaking grizzly bear. A monster. Was I even human enough to have any kind of relationship with her, or was what we'd just done all wrong?

She wasn't in any place to get attached to a man like me. How, after everything she'd been through, would she be able to survive me and what I'd become?

My goals were simple. I had to help her, not ruin her. Helping her was the only thing that kept my mind on the edge of hell instead of rolling in the flames. I had to leave her better than I found her.

I couldn't let myself be the fire that burned her up.

Chapter Eleven
Mira

I closed my eyes in anticipation of the softness of Caleb's lips against mine, but it didn't happen. When I opened them, I saw a slight frown flit across his features before he set me back in the passenger's seat and pulled my dress back over my legs. Maybe I had misjudged him. My inexperience with men would back that theory.

He threw the truck in drive and turned the radio up until the noise level was almost uncomfortable. I had done something wrong, that much was clear. I just didn't have a guess as to what. He didn't put his arm across the back of the bench seat as he often did, and I stayed firmly mushed up against the window, drowning in my confusion.

I leaned forward and turned the radio off completely. "What did I do wrong?"

Caleb rubbed his lip with the back of his hand until the rasp of his scruff could be heard. "I found a journal."

Utterly confused, I asked, "What journal?"

"I wanted answers about what I am, so I searched the old house at the back of my property for anything that would help me. Eli used to live there, so I thought maybe he would've left some clues or literature or something. All I found was a journal. Half the time I couldn't read his damned writing, but the other half told me enough to scare me off wanting a relationship with anyone. Do you understand?"

"You regret what we just did?"

"Yes."

The word felt like a slap to my face. "That was my first time…" I sighed and tried again. "That was the first time I had intimacy with a man, Caleb. And now you're taking it back?"

"I shouldn't have been your first anything."

"Why not?"

He hunched like the volume of my words were painful to his ears, but so what? He was breaking me apart right now.

"I can't have kids, Mira. I can't do it. They would be like me. You deserve better than a dead end relationship with a monster, okay?"

"I don't care about that—"

"You will. Someday, if I were to let this go, you'd want a babe at your breast, and I can't give you that. Not ever."

My heart was shattering. Was he right? If I let myself love him, really love him, someday I might want a baby who looked like him. Maybe he was smart to cut us off before we began. I didn't know. All I knew was right now his pushing me away was breaking my heart in two. "Caleb," I whispered as a warm tear slipped down my cheek.

He leaned forward and turned on the radio again.

****

Clint McCreedy lived just outside of town in the opposite direction of Castle de Fletcher, which gave me just enough time to collect myself and put my game face back on. Sure, my entire world had turned upside down, but I wasn't about to let Caleb's decision to dump me back into the friend zone ruin my life. If he didn't want me like that, I wasn't going to beg for his affection.

As we pulled up to the sprawling, Victorian style home, I tried my best not to gawk. It was light green with white trim and a porch that wrapped around the entirety of the giant home, complete with rocking chairs and an old dog lying on its back with four furry paws flopped into the air.

"Is your dog dead?" I asked, squinting to see if it was breathing.

"He always sleeps like that," Caleb said as he pulled the truck to a stop by a huge oak tree.

I hopped out before he could make it around to open my door. At the moment, I didn't want him doing something nice for me. I was still angry about our awkward encounter and uncomfortably silent car ride.

"Come on," he clipped out as he headed for the house.

I steadied my breath and pressed the wrinkles out of my dress with my shaking hands. I pulled a modest cotton cardigan I brought with me over my shoulders. It would be multi-functional in keeping me warm and hiding my scars. Movement caught my eye. An old wooden swing swayed gently in the cool breeze. It made me smile to imagine a much younger Sadey and Caleb pushing each other on it.

"You want to take her for a spin?" Caleb asked from right beside me.

He'd startled me, and from the amused look on his face, it was likely what he meant to do. This was his apology, making the effort to ease our discomfort.

"You would make a scary good hunter," I said of his stealth.

His eyes grew stormy. "Actually, I've come to realize I make much better prey."

His tortured gaze was so familiar. I had seen it reflected in the mirror often enough. The scars that Eli had given him ran much deeper than the visible marks on his skin.

"Push me?" I asked.

He wiped off the seat of the swing with the sleeve of his shirt and leaned against the tree until I situated myself onto it. And then he pushed. We didn't say anything but it wasn't uncomfortable silence anymore, and I was thankful that he had moved on from his ambivalence.

The old tree creaked the swing's rhythm, and I imagined the sound etched into the bones of this place. How many hours had he and his siblings spent swinging here?

As if he could read my thoughts, he said, "My father hung this swing for my mother before any of us were born."

I slowed and then stopped, hanging onto one of the ropes and twisting to better see his face. He walked around the front, relaxed onto the ropes with his hands, and looked down at me. From this angle, with the sun behind him and the strong lines of his jaw so close, he was utterly consuming.

"What was your mother like?" I asked.

Caleb looked far away, though his eyes stayed on me. "She was smart and funny. I can't really remember what she looked like anymore if I don't see her pictures," he admitted. "In pictures, she looks like Sadey."

"At least you have pictures of her," I said, leaning my face against the rope and wishing neither of us had to struggle with such a reality.

"You don't have pictures of your mom?" he asked seriously.

I shook my head. "When my memory goes, I'll have nothing left of her." I wouldn't tell him that I wished to forget her already. It hurt to think about my brightest memories of Mom. The ones at the end tortured me, and I was better off without them. That was my secret, and after what happened in the truck, Caleb hadn't earned it.

"You guys coming in or what?" Sadey yelled from the front porch.

Caleb pulled away and the swing groaned its relief at the release of his weight. "Ready?"

"Nope." I took his offered hand anyway.

He released my hand when I was safely up and walking, but he placed his hand gently onto the small of my back, and the gesture felt more comforting than I would ever admit to him. I would meet Clinton McCreedy, but at least Caleb would be right behind me.

For the first time in my entire life, I felt safe.

Mr. McCreedy met us at the door and graciously allowed us to pass into the sprawling entryway. Vaulted ceilings and a hanging chandelier that towered over us made the place feel cavernous.

It was hard not to look at Caleb's father. He was an imposing man who seemed to take up much more space than he actually did. He had a presence and a confidence that made me draw up and pay attention to him. He was tall and thin with dark hair, only just going a regal gray. His eyes were the same as his son's, but that's where their similarities stopped.

"Dad," Caleb said low, "this is Mira."

"Hello, Mira," Mr. McCreedy said, tilting his head. "You are a bit of a living legend around this town. Your reputation precedes you."

I smiled nervously and remembered that Sadey said to be honest. "I've heard a lot about you, too, but I assume your good reputation is deserved."

"So your reputation isn't, then?" he asked. His eagle sharp eyes captured me and dared me to look away.

"I'd like to think it isn't."

Mr. McCreedy's eyes narrowed as he studied my appearance. "That's a lovely dress. I seem to remember giving one similar to my daughter for her birthday."

"Dad," Sadey cut in. "You told me to donate what I wasn't going to wear anymore and that dress is too tight for me on top now."

Mr. McCreedy looked back at me, and I tried to hide my embarrassment. "You have excellent taste, Mr. McCreedy. This dress is the prettiest thing I have ever worn."

His look softened. "Let's eat, shall we?"

Caleb mouthed the words *I'm sorry* before we made it into the large dining room, but I shook my head demurely. It wasn't his fault, and besides, this was going way better than I thought it would. I had imagined Mr. McCreedy kicking me out before I made it up the front steps, so as far as I was concerned, we were in victory territory.

Brian was already sitting at the dining room table, and as soon as we sat down to eat, two older women in prim, dark suits brought out plates of food and set them in front us. I tried not to gawk at the whole fish that smelled delicious but looked back at me with an accusing eye. I pulled my attention to the dinnerware instead and played eeny-meenyminey-mo as I tried to figure out which fork to use on my meal before it chose to flop off my plate.

"Emily called and said she wouldn't be able to make it tonight," Mr. McCreedy said with a calculating look at me as I waffled between forks. "She has two tests tomorrow."

"She goes to college," Sadey clarified as she pointed subtly to the correct dining utensil. "Her classes are really hard this semester, and she has to study a lot."

"Speaking of studying," Mr. McCreedy said, "are you still homeschooling? I assume that is what your uncle was doing with you before he passed away. Sadey said you haven't attended public school in years."

"Oh, yes, sir. I just got my GED. I was supposed to graduate a couple of years ago, but my uncle struggled to keep up with the homeschooling. I am actually in the process of looking for full-time work now," I said, readying my fork to stab my meal.

Caleb cleared his throat from the seat beside me. "Dad, I actually wanted to speak to you about that."

Mr. McCreedy looked at Caleb suspiciously and interrupted his train of thought. "I got a call from Mike Wells, over at the big drill, who had some interesting news for you."

Caleb froze with his glass of ice tea against his lips. He spared a glance for me and then shook his head. "I don't want to discuss business at the table."

His father opened his mouth to say more, but seemed startled to a stop with the slamming of the front door.

"Family, I'm home," came a man's sing-songy voice.

I leaned over my plate to get a better look at who was tossing their jacket onto the polished floor like a slob when Mr. McCreedy answered him in a tone that lacked humor. "You're late."

"Not late. Making an entrance," Caleb's other brother Evan said as he entered the dining room. He stopped, his eyes growing wide before he gave a loud and humorless laugh. "What the hell is Crazy Mira doing here?"

"Evan—" Caleb warned him.

"She's with you? Ha," Evan said as he pulled out the chair directly across from me. "Now this I would have never seen coming in a million years. I'm eating dinner with Crazy Mira Fletcher," he said, grinning.

"Act like I raised you with manners," Mr. McCreedy scolded him, but Evan just kept staring at me.

I looked down, uncomfortable under his gaze. A plate clinked as one of the assistants placed it in front of Evan, but I could feel his focus remain regretfully on me.

"Damn, Caleb. Crazy Mira is kind of hot."

"Don't call me that." I was surprised to hear the steel in my own voice.

"Call you what? Hot?"

"Don't call me crazy."

Evan glared at me with a cruel twist to his lips. "If it looks like a duck and quacks like a duck."

Caleb slammed his fist on the table. "She said don't call her that. Do it again, and I'll lay you out, Evan. Don't fucking test me."

Evan looked completely unaffected by the threat of violence. Here was a man who thrived on chaos. He whistled long and low. "Sorry, little brother. You're so testy lately. I didn't know you were into banging handicapped chicks now."

"Enough," Mr. McCreedy ordered. "Mira is our guest. If you can't treat her with respect, you can leave."

Evan threw his hands in the air in apparent surrender. "Hey, I respect her. Who'd have thought under all of that hair there was a stone cold fox, huh, little brother?"

I could feel Caleb's tension beside me, and I rested the palm of my hand on his leg under the table. I'd never liked Evan, but he was Caleb's brother, and I hated to be the one to cause strain in a family. Plus, I was convinced he hadn't announced his bear status to his family, and he was getting dangerously close to his eyes glowing. He relaxed under my touch and squeezed my hand lightly in his own. Sadey passed me a bowl of light broth that she had spooned over her fish, and I pulled my hand regretfully away from Caleb's to take it.

Evan slouched down in my peripheral vision, and when his booted foot rubbed up the inside of my slightly parted legs, I jumped so hard I spilled the broth across my dress and part of Sadey's. In panic, I scooted the chair back, trying to escape Evan's wandering foot, and it made a screeching sound as wood scraped against wood. I gasped and looked down at my ruined dress in grief.

"Why did you do that?" Mr. McCreedy demanded, taking the half-spilled bowl away from my hands.

"I—" One look at Evan's sneering face had me frozen in place. Caleb was frantically trying to soak the broth off the front of my dress with his napkin when Sadey grabbed my hand and pulled me up.

"We'll be back," she said in a furious tone.

"Excuse me," I whispered to the chaos behind me. Evan's laughter trailed behind us as Sadey led me down the hallway and into a bathroom. I groaned in exasperation. This was even worse than my awful imaginings.

"Evan?" Sadey asked.

I nodded and looked miserably at the butter stain across my lap. Sadey disappeared and returned with a bottle of soda water and some cream-colored washcloths. She ran hot water and went to work to remove the stains. In an impressively short amount of time, only a wet spot remained, and Sadey turned her attentions to her own dress.

"Don't worry about him," Sadey said over the scrubbing sound. "He and Caleb have always fought. I think it is a jealousy thing for Evan. He's just trying to get to Caleb by messing with you."

"Well, he couldn't be more wrong. Caleb doesn't like me like that."

Sadey smiled to herself but didn't answer. When we left the bathroom, lowered voices could be heard from the dining room. Sadey stopped me out of view to listen.

"I think," Evan drawled, "what our old man is trying to say is that you have a reputation to uphold, and you are gallivanting all over creation with the biggest liability in town. And it's not just us who have noticed you are changing, Caleb. Ever since you met that girl, you've been a totally different person."

"I'd like to know what you are doing with her, Caleb," Mr. McCreedy admitted quietly.

"Nothing," Caleb said. "She saved my life. She needs help so I'm repaying the debt."

"Please," Evan sneered. "Don't insult us with that bullshit. You have never brought a girl around the family, and now you bring Crazy Mira? There is no way she's just a charity case for you."

"You don't have to worry about my reputation, Dad," Caleb said in a low, resigned voice, just loud enough for us to hear. "She doesn't mean anything to me."

The words stung like a slap to the face. We'd connected in the truck, and now I meant nothing? I'd completely misjudged Caleb's interest in me. I don't know why he had given into being physical with me if he had no feelings other than charity. Perhaps it was the bear inside of him that hurt his control. Or maybe that's just how men were—only interested in messing around. Maybe they didn't have to have feelings for a person to be intimate. I'd made a mistake giving anything to him.

The air caught in my throat, and Sadey looked at me with such sadness. I'd drawn my hand in front of my mouth at the shock of it all, but she pulled it down and squeezed it gently. She led me around the corner where Caleb sat with his head lowered, completely uninterested in his dinner. I couldn't quite take my eyes off the angry scars that curled out of the neck of his shirt. The men looked up at us with wide-eyed glances like they knew they had been caught.

Sadey grabbed her purse. "Come on, Mira. I'll take you home."

I nodded miserably. "Thanks for dinner, Mr. McCreedy. It was nice to meet you," I said softly, then followed Sadey out the front door without a spare word for the McCreedy brothers.

Hang them and their charity case. I didn't need anyone. Never had, never would.

I'd show them and make my own way.

Chapter Twelve
Mira

The next morning I woke early and put on my best outfit. Not the green shirt Caleb had bought me. That, I tossed into the back corner of my closet on principle. I had to find a job, and there was no way I was using any kind of letter of recommendation or help from any member of the McCreedy family. I didn't need anyone. It had been that way since I was a zygote. I was a natural born survivor, made to withstand trials that would bring others to their knees. I was a willow, fragile looking in its branches, but I could bend a hundred times over and not break. Or so I told myself.

I was shocked and blocked by a familiar truck on my winding, one-lane dirt road that would lead me to the front gate. Caleb looked just as shaken as me. He opened his door as if he wanted to talk but I pulled around him through the trees. I wouldn't stop him from paying whatever debt he thought he owed me, but I didn't have to make nice with a man who gave insults as easily as compliments either. I had shit to do.

I slammed my door after pulling into a parking spot on Main Street. I had thoroughly worked myself up on what I could have and should have said to Caleb after his flippant comments last night. My defensiveness wouldn't have solved anything, but the conversation in my head made me feel better somehow.

I hopped up on the curb and glared at Jake's Quickstop with determination.

"Hey Bernard," I said after I had marched through the front door, directly ignoring the obnoxious ding of the bell that announced my arrival.

Bernard looked up in shock, his hazel eyes widening at my direct greeting.

"Hey, Mira. What can I do for you?"

"Wanted to know if you were hiring. I can do anything, and whatever I don't know, I can learn. I can even help Leona in the kitchen if you need it."

Bernard opened and closed his mouth and opened it again. He looked like a fish out of water. "Sorry Mira, but we ain't hiring right now. It's a small store, and we have it covered between Leona and me."

He must have seen my face drop because he looked around, leaned forward, and lowered his voice. "Look, I wish I could help you out. If we had a spot for you, the job would be yours. I heard about someone hiring around here. She's new in town, but an odd bird, so I don't know if you'll even want to work for her. Name's Nelson. Opal Nelson, and she's opening up a pie shop at the end of the street. She's been having trouble finding help, or at least that's what I hear. Maybe go talk to her."

I smiled at his kindness and thanked him before I left.

Main Street was undoubtedly charming. It was lined on both sides with small stores and buildings with front porches and rocking chairs for passersby. While most of the buildings were painted quaint and subdued colors that looked picture-perfect paired with white trim and hanging flower baskets, the house on the end of the street was quite different. It was red. Not a subtle red, but lady-of-the-night lipstick red. The white trim only served to make the color look bolder. A huge *Grand Opening* banner was draped across the front of it in the loudest and tackiest font I had ever seen, each letter drawn in a different neon color. Headache inducing, if one looked at it for too long. It was a small, two-story building with a front porch and a balcony off the second floor. Small, two-person tables were set up on both levels and across the top story were the words *Main Street Pie & Candy Co.* in white paint. I eyed the front door warily as I read *Get Yer Buns in Here* across the window pane. A tiny picture of two butt-like cinnamon rolls had been painted right beside the signage.

I straightened my shirt and walked in. What else did I have to lose?

"Hello?" I called out. The room was well lit but no one could be seen. It smelled devastatingly good. Like fresh baked fruit pies, chocolate, and homemade bread.

"In here," a feminine voice called. "Come through the kitchen."

A glass display case took up most of the length of the main room, and it was minimally filled with a couple of cakes and a basket of French rolls. I had never actually seen anything from France, but the tiny sign in front of the basket said so. To the side of the glass was a counter that could be lifted. It creaked loudly as I entered the kitchen area, the obvious source of the rich smells. I heard a rustling sound in the back and followed it until I came to a small storage room.

The smallest woman I'd ever seen was standing precariously on a step ladder, reaching for a box of goods her too-short arms would never find purchase on.

I rushed to help her and pulled a box of cake decorating utensils down.

"Thanks, sugar tits. Put it in the kitchen, if you don't mind."

The way she spoke was confident and shocking. I liked her.

"If you're here for the grand opening, I'm afraid you are a day too soon," the older woman said, following behind me directly.

"Oh, no, ma'am. I'm here to see if you're hiring."

"You are? I mean, you are. Well, can you bake?"

"I've been cooking for myself since I was a little kid. Haven't done much baking, but not for lack of wanting. I'm a quick learn, though."

The woman grinned up at me from ear to ear. Her smile was infectious and I laughed. "Name's Opal," she said.

"Mira," I offered.

"When can you start?"

"Whenever you need me."

"Good. Put on an apron. You don't have anywhere to be today, do you?"

I stiffened in shock. I was employed. A tiny pessimistic part of me thought it would never happen. My happiness was quickly stamped out by an inconvenient guilt.

I sighed. "Ms. Opal. You are new in town and just starting your business. I don't know if I would be the best fit for you."

"Well child, why ever not?"

"People around here think I'm crazy. Or a witch."

"Are you?"

"No. Not that I'm aware of."

The woman scrambled up onto a stepladder near a countertop strewn with flour. She squinted at me for a long moment. "I believe you, and besides, I'm more interested in your work ethic." She poked my arm and then squeezed around the bony bits. "I'll pay you minimum wage," she said, taking on a professional tone. "It's all I can do right now, but you'll get a meal for lunch everyday on me. Ewey! Try this."

Opal shuffled to a large refrigerator, more quickly than I would have thought she was able. She pulled out a plate with a sandwich on top and handed it to me. I didn't know what to do with it.

"Well, don't just stare at it. Eat it. I'm thinking about putting it on the menu."

I bit into it. Surely, angels served sandwiches like this one in heaven. It was made on one of Opal's French rolls and had several different cuts of deli meat, some sort of cheese I couldn't even guess at, bacon, avocado, and a sauce that I had never come close to tasting before.

Opal watched me chew and lit up. "It's good then?"

I nodded earnestly. "Can I have the rest?" I asked around a giant bite.

"Of course you can. What do you think about the spread? I made it myself."

"Ith glor-e-ous," I said slowly. Hopefully, she understood food talk.

"Grab that." She pointed to a large menu sign that hung from the ceiling. It was written in colorful chalk, and when I had wrestled it off of its chains, Opal erased some of the writing under *Sandwiches* and rewrote the new one into it.

"I will need you to come in at five in the morning," she said. "Is that going to be a problem?"

I shook my head and popped a piece of bacon that had slid out of the sandwich into my mouth.

"Good. I hate early mornings so you'll be opening up the shop to start baking every day. As soon as you are confident in the kitchen, I won't be coming in until nine to help out with the breakfast rush. Apron," she said, pointing to a row of hooks.

I snatched off the largest one and tied it on before heading to the sink to wash my hands.

I turned around to find Opal holding up a bag of flour. "Lesson one."

Chapter Thirteen
Caleb

I couldn't shake the awful feeling I had about what I'd said last night. I couldn't decide if I felt worse about them being a lie, or about Mira having heard them. Of course, she meant more than nothing to me. Every time I changed into the damned grizzly, I crept up to her house like a stalker and watched her work outside just so I could feel connected to something from my old life. She was my most coveted anchor right now. It was in her best interest to stay naive of that, though.

I spent the majority of the day working on her dilapidated roof. The other repairs would be worthless if it kept leaking everywhere and causing more wood rot every time the clouds opened up. I took my shirt off in the heat of the day. It was cool, but between the physical exertion and frustration with myself, I had worked myself into an inferno. I would be able to see her truck coming from my vantage point, so I'd just shimmy down the ladder and cover my scars back up before she arrived.

I checked the road for the billionth time and shook my head. The more I told myself not to look for her, the more I did. And the longer she took in town, the more worried I became. What errand could she have that would take the entire morning and most of the afternoon?

I slid my hammer into the tool belt draped around my waist. The wooden handle made a soft zipping sound as it fell into the leather loop made for it. I scooted over the weather-rotted shingles and cranked the radio I had hauled up here as loud as was comfortable to my oversensitive ears. Water to drown out thoughts of Mira.

A Slipknot song blared. It wasn't usually the type of music I enjoyed, but it created an unavoidable distraction and an intense beat to work to. I wiped my brow and made an unattainable goal for myself to finish half of the roof before the sinking sun robbed me of essential light for the job. I was good under pressure and liked a challenge.

Hours of racing time did, indeed, keep my thoughts focused. The sun was a half circle that promised to disappear behind the horizon when I finally stood up and stretched my aching back. I watched it sink slowly behind the trees. The moment would have been profound if I hadn't realized hours ago that I left the pain meds in my jacket pocket in Brian's truck. The half-healed remnants of my fight for life screamed their existence.

The music cut off mid-song, and I frowned at the old radio in confusion.

"Roof is looking really good, Caleb," Mira said from behind me.

I turned and crouched to keep my balance. She stood on the ladder so only her face and shoulders were visible. She tossed the extension cord that had powered the radio to the ground below.

"Hand me the radio, and I'll take it down for you," she offered.

I looked around in panic. I felt naked without my shirt. Before the bear, I would have never thought twice about taking it off, but these days, my self-consciousness was a dark and unwelcome companion.

"What's wrong?" she asked.

"Nothing. I just…can you give me a minute?" I crossed my arms over the biggest scar. It wasn't enough to cover them all, though. Not by a long shot.

She furrowed her brow and raked her eyes across my marred flesh. "Okay," she said quietly.

I didn't miss the hurt in her tone, and it made me angry to care so much about it. I couldn't seem to stop hurting her. Maybe if she wasn't so fragile. I needed somewhere to place my blame, and I rubbed my face with the realization that I didn't really like what I had become. Not just the bear part of me, but the man I was turning into. I cursed under my breath and left the radio on its perch by the chimney. The weather was steady, so the roofing supplies would hold until morning.

The last rung of the ladder groaned as I hopped off and looked around for Mira. She must have gone inside. I hesitated. I should leave right now and let her be, but I'd never get to sleep tonight if the last thing I showed her was impatience. The gnawing ache inside of me begged to right the wrongs that had come from my mouth yesterday. After I threw my tool belt in the passenger seat of the work truck and pulled my cotton T-shirt firmly over my chest, I knocked softly on the frame of her door.

She stuck her head out of her bedroom. "You leaving?"

"Yeah, I'm gonna head out. I'll be back tomorrow to finish the roof."

"Okay. I got you something."

She grabbed a brown paper bag off the kitchen counter as I stood in her doorway.

"Figured you'd be starving," she said as she handed it to me.

"You didn't have to get me anything, Mira." The bag made a crinkling sound as I opened it, and a delicious smell wafted out of the inside. It was a gourmet sandwich with a bag of potato chips. "Where did you get the money for this?" I asked her, regretting the words as soon as they left my lips.

Mira lifted her chin up. "I earned it."

I searched her face to see if she was joking. Sometimes I couldn't tell with her. She seemed serious enough, and I was distracted by the line of white that graced one of her cheek bones. Upon closer inspection, I noticed the white powder covered most of her. I resisted the urge to wipe the smear off with the pad of my thumb. How could I think of doing that after what I'd said last night?

"You hurting?" she asked with a worried set to her full lips.

I nodded. "Forgot my meds today."

"I found some Advil in my uncle's medicine cabinet. It won't help much, but maybe it'll take the edge off."

I moved stiffly for the kitchen table. "Sounds good. Mira," I said, grabbing her hand before I could stop myself. "I'm sorry."

She froze and looked at our touching palms with wide eyes. "Don't," she said, prying her hand from my grip. "You don't have to do that, Caleb. I'm your charity case, remember? You were honest with your father, and I have no interest in ruining your reputation. Don't confuse me now."

I waited long enough to make the silence between us awkward. "Probably best if I go." Now, I definitely regretted the decision to come after her.

"Probably best," she agreed.

I turned back at the door. "How did you earn the money? For the sandwich, I mean."

"I got a job," she said with a proud tilt to her chin. "And without anyone's help. I'll be working mornings so you won't have to see me most days."

I tried not to let the disappointment show on my face. Not about the job. I was so proud of her accomplishment. The idea of not seeing her anymore, however, curdled in my gut. "Congratulations. Where at?"

"You're looking at the newest baker at the Main Street Pie & Candy Co.," she said with a smile and a little curtsy.

"That's great, Mira," I said, holding up the sandwich bag. "I'll tell the boys at the rig about it. Maybe drum you up some business. Goodnight."

"Night," she said with a sad smile. "And Caleb?"

I turned. "Yeah?"

"Your scars don't bother me." She looked down, face flushed. "They are proof you are a survivor."

What she said made me angry. I don't know why. Maybe because I didn't feel like a survivor. What kind of survivor dreamt about his tormentor every night? What kind of survivor never moved on? Or maybe it was because she had acknowledged the scars. I'd never given much effort for vanity, but my ruined flesh and my inability to escape the whispers and stares was something that had settled stubbornly into the darkest parts of my soul. They were a constant reminder that I was more animal than man now.

"Why do you hide your scars then?" I asked her. I watched her eyes turn angry and her lip tremble with unspoken words she was too kind to say.

"Because I didn't survive mine," she said. Mira turned and disappeared into her room, slamming the door behind her.

I knew what she meant. She thought she was broken from whatever had happened. She thought the best parts of her had been lost in whatever tragedy had marred her body.

She thought she knew, but she didn't.

The survivor between us was crying softly in her room.

Chapter Fourteen
Mira

Four o'clock came early, and I struggled out of bed. I would need to get on a better sleeping schedule. I had gone to bed early in hopes of being well-rested for my second day of work at the pie shop, but thoughts of Caleb kept me up. Kept me angry.

He was trying to hurt me, but I couldn't figure out why.

Had I been wrong about him?

Maybe he was just like everyone else.

Perhaps it was my fault for thinking so highly of him.

I had set myself up for the disappointment, not him. My current hurt was all on me for trusting a stranger. For trusting anyone.

On and on my thoughts tumbled until, at last, I had fallen into a fitful sleep a couple of hours before I needed to wake up.

The town was hushed when I arrived at the bakery. The street lights lit the dark before dawn with somber halos of yellow and white. The air was still as the town slept. I had never seen it so quiet, so otherworldly. It felt tranquil.

One step into the bakery and the chaos that contrasted the peace outside was a shock. Opal was worse at mornings than I was—by a lot.

"Start brewing the coffee. That will be the first thing you need to do every day," she clipped out as I shut and locked the door behind me.

She wore electric blue pajama bottom pants and a shirt that read *kiss me, it's my birthday*. A tired frown peeked out from under her glasses. Opal showed me how to brew coffee and then oversaw as I baked croissants, French rolls, fresh-made bagels, and muffins. When the breakfast items were in the oven or cooling, we started lessons on the dessert items we would need for the day. Pies, cheesecakes, cookies, chocolates. Opal had a way of doing everything faster. Every item to bake, she had down to a science. She had her recipes carefully written out, but she didn't need them. Every ingredient she told me from memory while I scoured the instructions.

I stayed in the back as the first customers ambled into the shop around eight. My idea. I didn't want to scare off business, and Opal had a way of talking to people that left them with a smile when they walked out the door with their bag of breakfast. She was kind, but with a wicked wit. She had a foul mouth and a dirty mind, but she joked in such a manner that people wanted to figure her out, not snub her. The curiosity with her small stature was also something that seemed to bring people in. No one asked her about it, but plenty stared. Opal, as it turned out, was a professional whisper-ignorer. I watched her closely and realized she didn't take anything that anyone said seriously because she didn't take herself too seriously. She was impossible to figure out. She could be the most confident woman in the world or the most insecure, but I hadn't a guess. She was self-deprecating, but in a way that begged a laugh.

"Vertically challenged coming through!" she would say when she needed to refill the coffee lids. Or when an old friend came in and joked that he would open another bakery next door, "Horace Jenkins, just because I have to stand on a stepstool to kick your ass, doesn't mean I won't do it!"

"Pixie high five!" she said, when she tasted the lime mayo I had whipped up. Except she didn't wait for me to hold my hand up. Instead, she smacked the back of my locked leg and it buckled under me. I grabbed the counter to right myself, much to Opal's cackling amusement. I smiled but didn't turn around. She didn't need the encouragement.

"Mira, take the register," Opal chirped when we ran out of her special sandwich sauce in the middle of the booming lunch rush.

"I don't think that's a good idea," I whispered.

"Course it is. I'm faster at making it, and you need to learn to take the orders. Hup, hup." Opal shooed me to the front counter and scrambled to the ingredients station.

I wiped my hands on my apron and smiled uncertainly at the next person in the long line. "Can I help you?"

"Hey, you look familiar," the older gentleman said with a slight frown.

The clean clothes, ponytail, and makeup were probably throwing him off.

"I'd suggest the Finger Lickin' Good," I said, ignoring his scrutiny. Opal had been creative with naming her sandwiches.

He cleared his throat and shook his head. "No, I'll have the Monday Funday with chips and a drink. Can you make that to go?"

I wrote his order down. "Sure thing," I said as I punched the price into an oversized, purple rhinestone calculator and figured out the tax. Opal didn't put much stock in computers. Instead, she had a red antique cash register that had been refurbished. I counted out his change and thanked the powers that be that I had finished my schooling. Math wasn't my strong suit, but I was able to do this much comfortably. When I turned around to add his order to a clip on the counter, Opal gave me two thumbs up with an over animated grin on her face. I turned back to the register with a smile, which disappeared right from my face when I saw who our next customer was.

"Crazy Mira?" Becca asked, her perfect pout thinning as her eyes narrowed. She turned to the rest of the line. "Crazy Mira works here. I don't know about you guys, but I don't want to eat food made by a witch." She slid her purse off the counter and sashayed out the door.

Everyone froze. And stared. And then talked in a hushed whisper. Half of the line headed for the door.

Opal cursed softly behind me. "Well, sugar tits, we knew this was coming. Help me up."

She dragged a stepstool to the register, and I helped her scramble up onto the counter. She let out the most ear-splitting whistle I'd ever heard, and the crowd heading for the exit halted.

"Listen up, you small-minded nutsos. Yes, Mira works here. She is a great cook and a hard worker. I know you have predisposed notions about her, and no matter what I say, you will leave, anyway. But I run a spotless shop. She's had a hard life, and I'm a little person. So what? Doesn't make us any less able to make the best damned sandwiches you ever put in your pie holes."

The majority of the crowd still filed out the door.

"Sandwiches are half off for the rest of the day. Tell your friends," Opal sang after them.

To the townspeople's credit, some of them stayed to collect their discounted meal. And some of them talked to me like I was a human being, which felt like a huge win.

"I'm sorry," I told Opal as soon as the rush died down.

"Don't you dare apologize for that," she said before she smacked my butt and jerked her head toward the door. "You did good today. Now grab a sandwich and get on. I'll see you in the morning."

"If you have to let me go, I understand," I said, giving her a way out of this. "As soon as they figure out none of their friends sprouted demon horns from our food today, they'll be back. They'll have to get used to you sooner or later."

****

Opal leaned back in her chair and chewed on a pen thoughtfully. "You going to the Founders Parade?"

I swallowed the last bite of my salad wrap and ripped a bag of potato chips open. A couple of them spilled onto the table, and I picked them up and popped them into my mouth. I snorted. "Why would I?"

"Well, why not? Have you ever been?"

"Yeah, I tried to go with my uncle one year. Let's just say it was a memorable experience. And not in a good way." I pushed the memory of Uncle Brady's public, drunken fistfight, subsequent arrest, and night in jail out of my head. It had been one of many unfortunate adventures with my guardian. "Plus, I'd be uncomfortable sitting with all of the townies. I'm pretty sure they feel likewise."

"You'll come to the parade and sit up on the second story of the pie shop. It'll be the best seat in town. The parade will go right past here. Oh! You could invite that McCreedy girl to sit with us."

Sadey had bought sandwiches from the pie shop three times this week to show her support. She even managed to drag her father in over the weekend. By the shock on his face, I was pretty sure she hadn't told him I worked here. From the dreamy looks Opal threw the man all during his lunch, it was obvious she had developed a crush on a McCreedy, too.

"You just want to lure Mr. McCreedy to your shop again," I accused around a mouthful of chips.

"Can you blame me? That man is fine. I bet he tastes like licorice."

I scrunched up my nose and pushed the rest of my chips toward her. "Gross."

"Payday," she said, tossing an envelope across the table to me. "Tell me you're going to spend your money partying."

"Yep. A paint party for one. I want to start painting the outside of the house tomorrow. I'm thinking red," I said with a wicked grin.

"I approve. Of the color, not the painting party. I can't name anything I would hate doing more."

I stood and threw my trash away in the garbage can by the door. "Being elected mayor of an all-woman town?"

Opal squinted at me. "Touché."

"See you Monday."

She waved. "Enjoy your day off."

My shift had ended a couple of hours ago, but I had stayed to help

Opal close up. It was the perfect excuse to avoid Caleb. It was the last day before he started work back on the rig, and for the past week and a half, I had done a grade-A job of avoiding the man. From the way he cut out early every day, I thought he was probably playing a similar game.

I could tell he put in a full day's work when I came home every evening. The house was coming along. New roof, plumbing didn't leak, all of the rotted boards in the house had been replaced and were awaiting a fresh coat of paint. The gutters worked again, the chimney no longer sat at a forty-five degree angle, the horse's shelter had been expanded into a small barn, and I didn't fall through the holes of my front porch anymore, which now boasted a new swing. I couldn't believe Caleb had done it all in such a short amount of time. I was suspicious he had brought help with him to finish what he had felt compelled to do before he started back to work. I didn't even want to think about how much he had spent on materials or labor.

After I cashed my paycheck, I headed for the hardware store a couple of buildings down. Red wasn't my style. Good thing, because the store only had about five colors of readymade paint in stock. The mixing machine had a sign across it in masking tape that read *out of order*. White was fine with me, and the shutters would look good in dark blue. I grabbed a couple of paintbrushes and paid for my wares. Pride filled me when I didn't have to worry about having enough.

The man behind the counter looked over his glasses suspiciously at me. "Don't take that cart out with you."

A man in his late thirties took a cart filled with bags of cement out the front door.

"Why not?"

"Because I said so. I don't want my cart disappearing on me."

I clicked my teeth closed with an audible snap. "You think I'm going to steal your cart?" I couldn't tell if I was more angry or hurt.

The man crossed his arms and stood up to his full height. I wasn't intimidated. "Whatever," I grumbled. "I'm going to have to make a few trips."

He nodded tersely but didn't offer to help. I shoved the paintbrushes in my pockets and grabbed the first two cans. They made a loud clunk as I set them firmly into the back of my truck, then stopped short when I saw a familiar silhouette disappear into the hardware store. Hesitating, I bit my lip and stood behind the safety of my old rusty truck. I couldn't just leave my paint in there. I'd already paid for them, and I knew the guy working the counter wouldn't save them for me. I'd just wait until Caleb came back out. Years of hunger had instilled patience as one of my few virtues.

The salesman inside talked to Caleb amicably. They laughed at something he said, and then the asshole pointed an accusing finger directly through the window at me.

"Shit," I whispered. I ducked down out of sight, but not before I saw the look of surprise on Caleb's face as he searched the store window.

He found me squatted down behind my truck, biting the corner of my thumbnail and hoping he would let me be.

"Hey," he said through an amused grin. "Who are you hiding from?"

Honesty was the best policy. "You."

His face darkened, and he looked away. I used his distraction to jump up and skirt around him. The cans of paint were solid in my hands, and I turned to run directly into Caleb's chest. He steadied me with a strong grip. In my haste, I hadn't realized he followed me back into the store.

He grabbed the last four cans. "Let me help."

The man behind the counter glowered at Caleb, but I ignored him. "Suit yourself."

After he finished securing the paint in the back, I hopped in my old Green Monster. "Thanks for the help. I mean with everything. The house looks—well, it looks like a home again."

He shut the door and gripped the open window. Inch by inch, he leaned closer to me. "Mira, listen—"

A group of men ambled across the sidewalk in front of my truck, talking loudly. "Caleb!" one of them called. "You coming to Rooney's? Beer's half off for the game."

Caleb nodded a greeting. "Yeah, I'm right behind you."

A few of the guys squinted, as if they were trying to decipher who Caleb was talking to in the ugly truck, but they kept moving. Caleb inched away. "I guess I should go."

I tried to keep the bitterness out of my voice. "Right. On account of your reputation and all." The engine roared to life as I gave an angry twist of the key. He opened his mouth to say something, but I jerked out of the parking spot before he could. I didn't want to hear it.

In another lifetime, I had self-esteem. I had a life. I went to school, had friends, and felt worthy of affection. Everything had been leached from me. Snuffed from my life to make it dark and barely livable. But now things had changed, and I began to think I deserved something. Anything. It was Caleb's fault for giving me wants again. My life had been fine when I'd felt nothing but desperation for my next meal.

A life void of feeling hurt less.

Chapter Fifteen
Mira

Indian style. Where had that term come from? It was the most uncomfortable sitting position for someone with very little cushion in their backside. Though my diet had improved tenfold as of late, my butt bones still threatened to pierce through my paper-thin skin. Maybe I should have studied harder in anatomy. I was pretty sure *butt bone* wasn't a scientific name.

Paint splattered my leg as I swept the paintbrush across the wooden siding on the front porch. It was a crisp morning, cool as a fresh spring and not weather-fit for cut-off jean shorts, but there was no way I was going to ruin any of my new clothes painting the house. Two hours in and my arms were already shaking with fatigue. Breakfast hadn't helped much. My stamina was still unimpressive, was all.

The noise of an approaching car made me hunch my shoulders against the dread. Caleb shouldn't be here. He was starting work on the rig today. It would be his first day back. I had counted the days with a mixed sense of apprehension and relief.

Like Sunday.

When I was young and still in school. Sunday was both my favorite and least favorite day of the week. It was the weekend, but the last day of it. Saturday night I would ready for Sunday and think, *phew, another day before I start back to school.* But in the next breath I would think, *only one more day until I start back to school.*

It was the same feeling with Caleb.

No longer would he come over and work on my house. I didn't have to avoid my home or the man who held my emotions in his careless hand. I also wouldn't have a chance to see him, and my house would feel emptier without proof of his being there.

I turned slowly. Sadey's little green hatchback made its way up the dirt road. A shaky breath of relief escaped my parted lips, and I waved with the paintbrush.

Sadey shut the car door, and it echoed into the emptiness of my land below. "Caleb said you could probably use some help today."

If only the sound of his name didn't cut a slice through my middle. "You want to use your Saturday to help me paint?"

She shrugged and grabbed a paintbrush before she wrestled her cellphone out of the back pocket of her jeans. "I'm grounded. Dad said the only acceptable reason for me to leave the house would be manual labor. I told him a friend needed help painting. I have to send him pictures on the hour, every hour." The phone clicked as she smirked in front of it with a paintbrush placed below her nose like a mustache.

I stood to unscrew the shutter closest to me. "You could paint the shutters so we can get them drying in the yard if you want. What are you grounded for?"

"Broke curfew. By, like, ten minutes. He's freaking out. You're so lucky you don't have anyone bossing you around."

I didn't agree but didn't say so. Her dad loved her. He wouldn't stress about her curfew if he didn't. I would have given my kneecaps to have someone care about me in such a way. She didn't need to be reminded about how pathetic my life was, though. Sadey just needed someone to listen while she vented.

I turned on the radio Caleb had left behind, and we got to work. The time passed a lot more quickly with the easy conversation Sadey provided, and by the time the sun hung halfway over the horizon, we had finished three sides of the house. The back was the only side left bare. We stood back and admired our work.

Sadey picked paint off her hands while she surveyed the improvement, and the corner of her mouth turned up in a satisfied grin. "Not too shabby, Fletcher."

"I'd live here."

Sadey snorted. "Please. You'd live in a rat hole and make it work for you."

"Hey, a rat hole is a home, too."

There was no comparison between the shack that had barely stood upright on my property three weeks ago and this house. It was no longer one and a half stories of moldy dilapidation. It was one and half stories of charming, invulnerable, homey abode. The front porch railings were whitewashed to match the house's siding, and the window frames were painted in the dark blue of the shutters. We had even given the front door a fresh coat. By tomorrow evening, the outside would be completely painted and finished. A tension that had settled directly into the middle of my back eased at the thought.

Sadey interrupted the serenity. "You coming to the Founder's Parade?"

"Why does everyone keep asking me that? I don't think anyone would appreciate me ruining their fun."

"I know someone who wouldn't mind you being there," Sadey said softly with her eyebrows arched.

"Who?"

"All I'm saying is Caleb is going to be in one of the floats. Well, not really a float. My brothers are riding with my dad in one of his fancy old cars."

I scrunched up my nose. "Your family has its own float?"

"All of the founding ancestors do. The Smiths, the Kleinfelds. The Hudsons have no living relations, but the Whitakers, Samsons, and McCreedys are still holding strong."

"Hmph," I said amusedly. "I guess my invitation got lost in the mail."

"Oh, my gosh. I totally forgot about the Fletchers. Whoa," she breathed. "That's so messed up."

I shrugged. I couldn't blame the town for excluding my family. Who wanted a float full of crazy people to ruin their parade?

"That settles it then. You are a founding ancestor. You should at least attend the parade."

I sighed in resignation. "Opal did invite me to sit on the second floor balcony of the pie shop. She said I could invite a friend."

"Fantastic. It'll be the perfect perch to spy on cute boys."

My boy-crazy friend and boss would be much more entertaining than any old parade. I looped an arm around her neck and leaned against her shoulder. "Come on into the shop before the parade. We're locking the doors at five till. I'll buy you a sandwich, and we can eat lunch while we watch."

****

Caleb

The hunger gnawed at me like a buzzard on a bone. Pain from my healing injuries was a constant, buzzing background noise, but after the first six hours of straining work, the ache of hunger overpowered it. I needed to eat a lot more now that I'd been changed.

The boys were taking me to lunch for my glad-you-didn't-die celebration. My boss had even given us an extra half hour so we could grab our grub in town. Unheard of before now, as a rig always kept rigorous hours, but hey, who was I to complain?

I popped a couple of pain meds into my mouth and downed them with a bottled water. The empty plastic container gave under the weight of my crushing hand. I didn't have to squish it to oblivion, but for some reason it made me feel better.

"Where do you want to eat?" Reyes asked.

"Oh, it's my choice, is it?" I pretended to think long and hard, but I already knew my answer. "I feel like trying somewhere new."

The boys and I piled into my truck and headed into town. There were six of us, which meant six opinions on what kind of music we should blare through the speakers. Evan flopped through the back window and stood up in the bed as we drove through town, legs splayed and holding on for dear life to the sides of the cab. He whistled at any girl on two legs. A part of me wanted to jerk the truck to a stop and flip him over the hood, but with him being my brother and all, I thought it a little too harsh a punishment for idiocy.

I hadn't been inside of the Main Street Pie & Candy Co., and I lifted my gaze to the diners relaxing on the second floor while they enjoyed their meal. If I could ignore the eye-maiming color of the outside, the place looked nice enough. Evan jumped out of the back of the truck and landed with a thud right in front of me.

"I know why Caleb picked this place," he said, loud enough for the boys to hear. "The waitress in here is a hot little piece of ass."

My blunt fingernails pressed into the skin of my palms as I imagined what it would feel like to put my knuckles through his teeth. If Evan knew anything at all, it was how to pick at a festering wound. And he did it for enjoyment.

Ignoring the guys and their obnoxious catcalls, I stepped around Evan. It was pointless to engage my brother. Years of arguing with him had taught me that.

I scanned the room for Mira as soon as we stepped inside and spotted her behind the counter. She had her hair pulled back. She wore a flour-covered apron and had an orange pencil tucked behind her ear. She looked thoughtful and polite and smiled shyly at old man Tucker as he put in his order.

"It's your party, little brother." Evan grinned at me with a predatory smile. "Why don't you and the boys take a load off, and I'll order us lunch. On me."

The disappointment that soaked my resignation was as uncontrollable as my heartbeat. He knew he'd taken my chance to talk to Mira away, and the dumbass all but skipped to the register as the others shouted their orders. Evan leaned against the counter, dripping with ego, and Mira's face fell when she saw it was him. I wished I could protect her from whatever utterly stupid thing Evan had said to draw her eyebrows down in anger.

"Hey, man. Have you heard anything we've been talking about?" Reyes asked.

I tore my eyes away from Mira and tried to pretend I hadn't just spaced on every single word that had been said since we walked through the door.

"Dude, there's Becca. Better run, McCreedy," Jeff snorted. "She'll have you married by nightfall."

I saw the recognition light up Becca's face as she saw us through the window, and I stifled a groan. It was too late to hide.

Becca came in and leaned into the chair behind me. "Can I talk to you?"

The boys made kissing sounds, but I ignored them. Instead, I nodded to Becca. I couldn't be rude to the girl in front of everyone. The chair made a scuffling sound as I pushed it back, and I caught the surprised look on Mira's face as I headed with Becca to the hallway for the bathroom.

"I was wondering if you would want to sit with me at the Founder's Parade?" she asked, getting straight to the meat of it.

Relief flooded me. I had a legitimate excuse not to subject myself to that uncomfortable hour. "Sorry, but I'm in the parade. I have to get back to the guys. We have a short lunch."

She grabbed my hand. "Please tell me you aren't here for her." Her whisper was pleading, and it grated on my last nerve. "I've been the only one to like you through all of your problems. I came to your mother's funeral, not her. I still care about you, even after that bear ruined you."

"Ruined me?" Sure, I felt ruined most days, but I never thought it was a deal-breaker for friends. Family. Girls. Apparently, I owed people who accepted me despite my marred skin. "Do my scars bother you that much?" I unbuttoned the top button of my old flannel work shirt, and when she looked around to make sure no one saw the red mark I had exposed, I undid another. And another. Her growing discomfort amused me.

"That's quite enough," she snapped as the last button was undone. "You're going to embarrass both of us."

She grabbed the flailing pieces of shirt and tried unsuccessfully to put them back together. I didn't help. I couldn't take my eyes away from her shame-filled blush at how torn and ragged my chest was.

"Excuse me," Mira said as she inched around us. "I just have to get to the bathroom." Her voice shook, and I glanced down to see what

Becca and I must have looked like to her.

"Mira, wait," I rushed out, prying Becca's hands away from my clothing.

"You don't have to explain anything to me. It's none of my business," she clipped out softly before she disappeared into the restroom.

Chapter Sixteen
Mira

I hadn't really needed to use the washroom. It was an excuse my fragile mind had made up to discover for myself the reasons Caleb had led Becca to the private hallway at the far end of the shop. Stupid mind and stupid excuses. I wish I could sear that vision of them together out of my brain for good. I'd do it with little remorse.

I splashed cold water across my face and patted it dry with a paper towel. A pale, shaken girl stared back at me through the mirror, and I turned my back in disgust. Weak. That man made me feel weak. Shoot a hundred and forty pound predatory grizzly with basically a water pistol and no fear of the consequences? No problem. See a nice boy canoodling with my arch nemesis? Crazy Mira falls to pieces. I chucked the paper towel into the trash bin like it had been the one to betray me. Caleb got to me. Didn't mean he deserved to see how badly.

Opal gave me a steady gaze over the top of her glasses when I slipped back behind the counter. "Food's ready for the big top. You mind taking it over to them?"

Caleb was staring at me. I could feel it so I didn't venture to look their way. "Can't we just call them up like we do with everyone else?" I whispered.

Opal arched her eyebrow. "If I'm not mistaken, I'd say there is a McCreedy or two at that table, and we need their shining endorsement. Now scat. You're harshing my mellow with your cloud of emo lovesickness. Your aura looks awful." She waved her hand in my direction like she was scattering fog and went back to slicing deli meat.

I opened my mouth with a ready denial but clicked my teeth back together again. She was right. I was full of emo-whatever-she-had-called-it. I shook my hands like coach was about to put me in the game and stretched my neck to the side until it popped. I could do this. They were just men. He was just a man. He was *the* man, but whatever. People had done far more difficult things. I mentally chanted those as I toted the giant tray of food over to their table.

Climbed Mount Everest.

Made a public speech.

Had more than fourteen seconds of conversation with Evan Dirty-Mouth McCreedy.

All much harder than I was about to do, really.

"Food's ready." My voice cracked, and I bit my lip when six pair of eyes swung my way. I could imagine the shade my face was turning.

Most of the boys kept talking, but Caleb had gone still and watchful. Evan moved gallantly out of the way so I could set the tray on their table.

"Evan," Caleb warned, a half second before I felt a firm squeeze on my left butt cheek.

"Told you she was a hot piece of ass," Evan sneered.

I gasped in shock as the force of his hand pushed me forward until I lay awkwardly on the table. I tried to right myself, but no one was looking at me anymore. Everyone's attention was riveted to the flurry of fists and violent motion that were making their way to the door.

I watched the raw fury on Caleb's face as he fought with Evan. Their friends herded them outside, but I could still see everything from my vantage point by the window. Caleb was beautiful. Vengeful. So graceful, he couldn't pass as human. Potent. I couldn't take my eyes off his agility as he pummeled his older brother with immoveable focus.

I had to stop them. This was over me, and I would never be able to live with myself if either really hurt each other.

I threw open the front door. "Stop! Stop them," I pleaded with their friends.

They only stood back with half smiles. Two of them were taking bets.

I lurched forward and grabbed onto Caleb's arm.

He saw enough of me that his tension eased, and he stepped back. His eyes were going to be impossible to hide if the gold in them kept spreading. "Mira—"

I saw it a split second before Caleb did. Evan wasn't as good a fighter, but the man made up for it by fighting dirty. "Watch out," I screamed just before his fist came flying in my direction.

Caleb yelled out. He pushed me behind him and took a hit directly to his face. Unbalanced and surprised by his strength, I fell backward into the crowd, the cement under me an unforgiving assailant.

"Hey," one of their friends said in disapproval as they held Evan back. "Not cool, man."

Caleb glanced back at me with worry etched into his bright eyes and blood trickling down his split lip.

"What do you care if I feel up the waitress, anyway," Evan spat. "Is she your girlfriend? Huh? Do you want to date her? Tell me! Do you have any claim on Crazy Mira at all?"

The street grew quiet as Caleb's shoulders hunched. I wished I could run away before the words left his lips. Caleb refused to look at me. "No," he said softly.

I nodded my head slowly. Of course. Why would I have expected a different answer from him? His need for a solid reputation hadn't changed since the last time we'd seen each other. Since the dinner with his father. Since ever. He was going to be someone. Maybe the biggest someone this sleepy little town had ever produced. I would be an anchor around his neck. Or if not me, the town's idea of Crazy Mira would be the brick that dragged him beneath his potential.

The only thing that could have made the situation worse came to fruition when I looked down to see my apron had come loose and sagged to the side. My shirt was disheveled and one still emaciated and angrily scarred hipbone stuck out for all to see.

"Freak," I heard someone murmur from the crowd.

My feet couldn't move fast enough as I scrambled for the safety of the pie shop. I sought my refuge in the inventory room.

Eventually, Opal ambled in and leaned against the doorframe to the tiny room. "You want to talk about it?"

My arms rested on my knees and my head on those. I shook my head slightly. My eyes were dry. I just didn't want to face the world quite yet.

"I'll be with you in a moment," she told a customer. Sitting beside me, she patted my arm. "At least tell me where you got the scars, Mira. That stuff is no good all bottled up. Tell one person and get it out of you. You can never move on if you keep that kind of darkness inside."

I couldn't bring myself to utter the words. Time dragged on, and I found the admission more and more difficult. When Opal stood to leave, I rushed the words, "I got them from being hungry."

Opal leaned her back against a row of shelves and waited.

"When I was so hungry I thought I would die, I had trouble getting around. I ran into things. Table. Bathroom sink. Dresser. Everything was right at the height of my hips. My bones stuck out so much and my skin was thin as rice paper. When I hit something, it would split me open, and I was too young to know how to stitch myself up yet."

Opal didn't offer advice or make sympathetic mewling sounds. She listened quietly with her hands clasped in front of her. "Go on home. Your shift is almost over, anyway, and the lunch rush has died down."

I stood and rubbed my sore bum.

"And Mira?"

I turned.

"The next time a man squeezes your ass without permission, lay him out. You understand?"

I laughed shakily. "Wouldn't that be bad for business?"

"Like hiring the town witch with a punch-happy throng of admirers following her around?"

I untied my apron and hung it on the hook. "Fair enough. Lay them out. Got it."

Opal sent me home with two sandwiches. I tried to refuse on account I didn't work the full day and hadn't earned either of them. She said my scars earned them for me. I could have sworn I saw her wipe moisture away from her eyes when she came out of the inventory room, but I've been known to be wrong before.

The oil workers had taken their lunch to go and headed back to the rig before I left the pie shop. Thank goodness for small blessings. If I never saw Evan McCreedy again for the rest of my life, it would be too soon. And Caleb? Well, I couldn't see the man soon enough but stilled my traitorous heart. I would just have to get used to the ache as I had done with everything else in my life.

****

"T minus five minutes and counting until the first float hits Main Street," Opal yelled over the street noise outside. "You girls lock up, and I'll take our food upstairs."

"You got it Ms. Opal," Sadey said. She snatched the keys from me and raced to the front door. "I win."

I rolled my eyes and tried not to smile. "Fine, race to the top floor." Even if she wasn't fumbling with the lock, I was much closer to the stairs and at an advantage.

"Cheater," she accused when she plopped down beside me at the table in the very middle of the balcony.

Opal was already divvying up our lunch, and the raucous crowd below was enough to provide plenty of entertainment for a curious people-watcher like myself. The whole town had shown up. I don't know why I was surprised. Everybody knew everybody, and this was the social event of the season. How much I had missed while sitting in my lonely tower on Dark Corner Road.

Sadey opened wide to shove a huge bite into her mouth in a very anaconda-like fashion but stopped mid-strike. "Caleb is on the seventh float."

I squinted at her as she delved into her ham and Swiss on rye. "Why would you think I need to know that?"

"Wait, wait, wait," Opal said. "Is Caleb the boy from the other day? Fists of fury?"

Sadey gulped. It was a miracle she didn't choke. "Sure is. I heard about the whole thing not ten minutes after it happened. Pretty sure the whole town did. I tried to call Caleb and get details, but he said he didn't want to talk about it and hung up on me. Lame. So then I thought about calling Evan, but you really can't believe a word that comes out of his mouth, so I called Caleb's friend, Joseph Reyes, instead, and he told me everything. Well, as much as he could tell me while riding in the bed of Caleb's pickup truck going sixty."

I crossed my arms. "Did he also tell you he was messing around with Becca in the hallway before he turned Kung Fu Caleb?"

Opal gasped and almost choked on a chip. "Mira, your life is like a movie."

I snorted. "A horror film."

Sadey crumpled up her trash and pointed down Main Street. "First float. And what do you mean *messing around* with Becca?"

"I mean, she was latched onto his completely unbuttoned shirt and their faces were an inch apart. He definitely looked like he was about to kiss her." Why did my voice drop to an embarrassing whisper on the last two words?

"Six more floats until Caleb's." Sadey air-balled her wadded up trash at the trash bin and missed it by a lot. She sighed and scrambled to retrieve it. "I suck at basketball."

"Yeah, honey," Opal said, scrunching up her face. "You do."

"You're pretty good at painting houses," I offered. "You know, if playing professional sports doesn't work out for you."

"Five more floats," Sadey said.

Darn my eyes as they searched for him.

Sadey pulled a bundle out of her purse. "I made these for us." She held out two tiny flags that read *McCreedy* in yellow script letters. One of them was spelled wrong.

"Homemade?" I asked.

"Shut up. You get the misspelled one for that."

We stood at the railing and watched the floats full of happy townspeople as they waved to the crowd below. Opal pulled up a chair and snatched the limp flag out of my hand.

"I'll cheer for a McCreedy," she said, stretching to see their float.

"I'm sorry, sugar, but your daddy is a spicy looking man." She lowered her voice and grumbled, "And Ms. Opal likes her sausage with a kick."

I groaned but Sadey laughed. "I'll tell him you said so."

"Please do so with relish." Opal waved her flag harder as the edge of the car the McCreedy's were driving peeked around the side of a huge float of a makeshift football field. A huge billy goat hung in mid-air, head-butting a giant football.

Sadey poked my elbow with her flag. "He likes you, you know."

"Who Evan? He doesn't like me. He just wants to boink me. Or at least that is what he told me before he got pummeled by your other brother."

Sadey sighed in exasperation. "The other brother is of whom I speak."

"Please. Caleb has made it clear, on several occasions, that I would ruin his precious reputation and that he doesn't have feelings for me. I embarrass him."

"Yeah," she conceded. "He hasn't handled things very well. You should have seen him at Sunday dinner. He was a mess."

I tossed her a worried look, and she smirked. "I knew it."

"My feelings have no effect on his feelings, Sadey," I reminded her.

Sadey shrugged and cheered, waving her tiny flag gallantly. I rested my forearms onto the wooden railing and swung my gaze to the refurbished Model T that made its way toward us in the street below. Caleb waved and nodded to people. He greeted old friends and acquaintances and shook hands with some of the older men who approached the car. Evan and Brian acted similarly in the back seat, and Mr. McCreedy waved and drove like a pro.

Even if I was mad at Caleb, I couldn't help the jitters that fluttered in my stomach when I watched him. I hadn't seen that smile before. He seemed relaxed, in his element. These were his people. The ugliest part of me let go of the lingering anger. Of course, he should stay away from me. He was right. His father and brothers were right. How could I be so selfish to think he should give up his relationship with his town in order to be with me? On top of everything else, Caleb had been honest with me from the start. He had never hinted with words that he cared about me as anything more than his project. His debtor. Not to mention, he was dealing with being a newly turned bear shifter. He had no room in his life for me. I'd been foolish to get so worked up over a man who had done nothing wrong—who hadn't led me on. The anger at myself was as sharp as the crack of a whip, and I bit my lip against the sting.

Caleb looked up, almost as if he could feel the turmoil roiling within me. Such a dark and turbulent feeling had to create some sort of brown and muddied aura around me surely. It couldn't be that he was so connected to me, though. His eyes held surprise. Then satisfaction. Then determination that rivaled the grizzly that maimed him. Caleb said something to his father and opened the door. The car was still in motion, and his father's shocked reprimand could be heard from where I stood.

"What the hell is he doing?" Sadey breathed beside me.

I hadn't a guess. He hopped out of the moving car and pushed through the crowd. The confounding man was headed straight for the pie shop.

He came to a stop right under me. "Mira Fletcher. Is there room for one more up there?"

My mouth hung open. I hadn't even the good sense to snap it closed.

"Oh, dear goodness," Opal whispered through a grin. "This is happening." She cleared her throat and spoke loud enough for him to hear. "Caleb McCreedy, the door's locked and we're not missing the parade to let you in. If you're going to do this, you better do it right. The fire escape will hold you."

Caleb grinned, and I was convinced that a heart could actually skip a beat if one was faced with a smile as capturing as his. Or maybe I was having a full-blown heart attack.

"He has lost his damned mind," I whispered as he grabbed onto the fire escape.

The town watched as Caleb scaled the bright red wall of the Main Street Pie & Candy Co. in order to seek out one Crazy Mira Fletcher. He hopped over the railing and wiped his hands off. His breathtaking grin had become bigger with the exertion. Sadey bounded out of the way when Caleb came to stand beside me. He was so close, I could feel the warmth coming off his arm.

"Well, you're in it now, Mira. You ready?"

I was highly suspicious. "Ready for what?"

"I'm going to kiss you."

I darted a glance to the waiting town below and then back to him. "But, I've never kissed anybody before."

Caleb leaned over and brushed his lips against mine. Softly. Slowly. More tenderly than I thought a man as powerful as him would be capable of. I couldn't pull away. I had frozen into place, and the warmth of his touch was the air I had been desperate to breathe. A salvation that loosened a trapped part of my soul. His mouth moved against mine, and his tongue brushed the closed seam of my lips. His fingers traced my jaw, and he stood, straightening me with him. His hands clenched my hair like I still wasn't close enough, and when my mouth parted for him, he dipped his tongue against mine. I felt like I was falling.

Easing back, his lips curved up into a smile. "Now you have."

Chapter Seventeen
Mira

I had been kissed. I had been *kissed*! Not only had I been kissed, but it had been by the most alluring man I'd ever met. It changed the way I saw our meeting in Jake's. Maybe he'd just been trying to help me but didn't know how and mucked it all up. He was a good man. The rightness that settled into my bones at the realization was overwhelming.

The parade below was a blur because Caleb kept touching me, and talking to me low, for only my ears.

"I wanted to protect you. I thought I was doing the right thing, but I can't do it anymore. I can't hurt you or stay away from you."

"Tell me you're the one who keeps dropping the fish on my doorstep," I whispered.

He brushed his lips against mine again and smiled. "I don't like seeing you hungry. My animal side doesn't either. I hunt for you every time I change."

"Will you tell me everything?"

His face fell. "It's hard to talk about. Is it something you need?"

"I think it's something we both need. Maybe you can tell me more about what you found in the journal, and then you won't have to be alone with all of this. I knew what you were before you did, remember? You can trust me with anything."

His eyes grew serious. "I know I can."

We leaned over the railing, and his warm hand rested on the small

of my back, rubbing it. This was really happening, and it was happening to me.
 I wanted to kiss him again.
 His lips were so sensual when he talked. He'd shaved this morning, and I yearned to reach out and touch his face. He felt like mine, so I did.
 Smooth against my fingertip, his jaw stretched with a slow smile. "You want to get out of here."
 "Yes," I whispered, too fast.
 A deep chuckle trickled from him as he stood straight, pulling me in until my cheek rested against his sternum. His heartbeat was racing mine.
 He was so warm, I stepped closer, burrowing into the blanket of safety he seemed to have enveloping him. His arms wrapped around my shoulders, and he rested his cheek against the top of my head. Dipping closer to me, his whisper tickled my ear and made my legs lock up. "I've been waiting a long time to do that. To kiss you."
 I eased back and frowned. "How long?"
 "Since I watched you shoot that grizzly over me." The sincerity in his eyes was so deep, I'd drown right here and happily.
 Memories of it stormed me like a battlefield. We'd fought for our lives together that day. "You mean since you saw my boobs?"
 His laughter was instant, booming, and his smile reached every facet of his face and landed in his dancing eyes. Leaning forward again, he said, "They're perfect."
 "Flattery will get you everywhere with me."
 He tilted his head, laughter still playing at his lips. "Come on. I want to show you something."
 Tossing Sadey and Opal a wide-eyed glance, I followed Caleb down the stairs. The parade had come to an end, so I opened the store and flipped the sign. Opal had assured me I could keep my day off, and she could handle the post-parade crowd, but I still felt a little guilty leaving. Up until the point when she hung over the balcony, catcalling like a maniac and waggling her eyebrows from above. Opal would be just fine without me today.
 Caleb wrapped his strong hand around mine, like it was the most natural thing in the world, and led me through the crowds. If anyone gave us dirty looks, I didn't notice. I was too enamored by his hand holding mine and the feeling of utter freefall that made flip-flops in my stomach. It was scary to admit how much I liked him—how much I needed him already.
 Caleb didn't slow until we reached the back of Bealls where he had parked the truck. Most of the parade goers seemed to be hanging

around Main Street. The smell of food carts and popcorn filled the breeze. When we were away from the masses, he pulled me up against his side and draped his arm over my shoulders. I'd never been drunk before, but this must be what it felt like. Caleb looked down at me with such adoration, my heart jumped, and my throat filled with all of the things I wanted to say to him.

At the door of his truck, he pressed his back against it and drew me in. Slowly, he lowered his lips to mine and drank me in. I melted into him, pressing and pushing until I was molded to the strong curves of his taut chest and stomach. This time wasn't so scary. It wasn't for show, and it wasn't my first, and if I was honest with myself, Caleb's lips already felt familiar. And I trusted him. He was strong and had obviously had practice doing this, so I let him teach me in that gentle way of his. I ached for more, for everything.

But when he pulled away, breath ragged, he looked at me like I was the one who'd taught him something, which baffled me. "In the truck, woman, before I lose my mind."

He pulled the door open and helped me up with an offered hand. And when I was settled, he reached across and buckled me in. Now, I could've done it myself easily, but he seemed to need to be close to me, to take care of me, and I understood. I felt it, too.

The belt clicked into place. He stood, searching my eyes for some answer I hadn't a guess at before his gaze dipped to my lips again. I laughed. Caleb was just as hungry for my touch as I was for his. The truth of it was written in the raw look in his eyes. The one that made my insides tremble to touch him again.

He pulled away with a grin, then shut the door. The truck rocked as he slid behind the wheel. As he pulled onto a dirt road behind Beall's, he slid a hand over my thigh and rested it there. His hand belonged there. How could a man who'd denied me his touch for so long feel so comfortable now? I looped my hand around his wrist and stroked comforting little circles to keep him in place, and he slid me a smoldering look before his eyes found the road again.

On and on we drove until we hit the winding road to his dad's house. I buckled against revisiting a place that had been so hard on us. Someday I would go back, but I didn't want to today.

"Caleb?"

"Don't worry. I'm not taking you to the house. I want to show you someplace I've never shown anyone before. My family will never know we've been here."

Caleb was letting me in. I didn't know how I knew it, but I felt it in my bones that he hadn't ever let anyone in like he was doing with me right now.

He pulled onto a dirt road that didn't look like it had been used in a long time. It was overgrown, and briars scratched against the undercarriage and sides of the truck, like Mother Nature didn't want humans in her secret garden. The truck rolled on, bouncing and jouncing until we reached a ravine.

I slid out of the truck and was awestruck. Cicadas sang, birds chirped, and bullfrogs croaked. The thick trees made a canopy that doused everything in shadows with the occasional sunray peeking through to the forest floor.

A river slashed through the land, winding this way and that, and the bubbling currents could be heard over the sound of the animals and insects.

"This way," Caleb said from beside me. He held onto my hand again, like he needed the connection to me, and led me up a small path. Under his other arm was tucked a folded blanket.

We climbed higher until we looked over the ravine, and at the top of the hill, under the shade of a giant oak tree, he smoothed the blanket onto the leafy ground. From here, I could see the river below and the town in the distance. The forest surrounding us was breathtaking.

My woods were home, but Caleb's woods were magic.

He sat and leaned against the trunk of the old tree, then held out a hand for me. I sat between his legs and relaxed against his chest.

"I used to come here when I was a kid," Caleb said low, like he didn't want to interrupt the bird song from the branches above. "Evan used to drive me mad, and I'd tear off for this place to get away from him. None of my family ever discovered it, as far as I know, but this was where I found peace. I didn't visit here at all after I moved out, but when I met you, I started thinking about it again. I've come out here a few times since the attack, just to clear my head, you know?"

I inhaled slow and tilted my head up. "I do that in my woods, too." I understood it more than he could ever guess.

"I was wrong, Mira. I'm sorry for hurting you and for making you feel unimportant. I thought if I could fight my feelings for you, that you'd be better off, but I can see how much I've hurt you."

"No more running."

He shook his head, eyes never leaving mine. "I'm in it now."

"No more secret trysts with Becca by the bathroom," I said with a mock frown.

"That," he said with a chuckle, "was just a really unfortunate case of bad timing. We weren't doing whatever it looked like. We were arguing."

"Mmm," I murmured, tracing the edge of the scar on his neck. "I want to argue like that."

His gaze dropped to the river. "You scare me."

The words hurt. I didn't want to scare him. All I wanted to do was make him happy. "I don't mean to."

He wrapped his arms around my chest and pulled me close. Inhaling deeply, like he was smelling my hair, he leaned his cheek against mine. "I know." The words rumbled against my back, and the soft brush of his lips against my neck made me shiver.

"What was that?" he asked, a smile in his voice as he froze against the sensitive skin of my throat.

"It feels nice when you touch me. I think about what we did in your truck a lot." The admission brought heat to my cheeks.

His breath shook as moments stretched on. I twisted, leaning my cheek against the tripping pulse in his throat. His eyes were a raging storm when I eased back, and he searched my face for something I couldn't fathom. Slowly, I lifted my lips to his.

His lips crashed onto mine with none of the patience or restraint he'd shown at the parade. Out here, we could be us, and right now, I didn't want gentle either. I wanted him to show me how much I meant to him without words. His mouth moved against mine, stroking, lapping, enticing my lips to open for him, and when I did, a helpless-sounding growl escaped his throat. His hands tangled in my hair, and then he turned me to face him. His tongue stroked against mine and made me yearn for more.

As he palmed the back of my head, the soft sound of his growl rattled against my ears. I relaxed my neck and let him have my lips. Commanding and powerful, he drew more and more from me until I was left breathless and wanting. His hand brushed my collarbone and trailed down to my waist, dragging fire as I wrapped my arms around the back of his neck. It still wasn't enough.

How long we stayed there like that, wrapped up in each other, I couldn't guess. The sun was lower, and clouds had come in from the east, but that seemed less important than Caleb's burning touch. He pulled my shirt to the side and kissed the circular scars, and I couldn't find it in me to care about the memories they caused. Caleb was healing me with his touch. With his mouth urgent against my skin, I moaned and gripped his hair as he reached the base of my throat.

"Caleb," I pleaded.

His arms tensed around me. "Did I hurt you?"

"I want more. I feel like I want—" God, what did I feel? Everything. Rightness. I wanted more of him, but what did that even mean? I tugged on his earlobe with gentle lips.

"Mira, I didn't come out here to take advantage," he rasped, his hands clenching my sides as I nestled even closer.

"Stop," I implored. "Words like that taint what this is. I know what I want, Caleb." As I straddled his lap, his breath hitched.

His hands ran up my back and gripped my shoulders, pulling me against him as I rocked gently.

"Shit," he gritted out, as I rolled my hips again. "Mira, we're not ready. This isn't how I want it for our first time."

My instinct was to feel the slap of rejection. I hadn't ever been intimate with a boy besides him, and insecurity told me I was doing this wrong. But then again, I liked the way he'd said that. "Have you thought about us together before?"

I raked my fingers through his hair, and he leaned back against the tree with a sigh. "Of course, I've thought about it." He grasped my hips in an almost painful grip. "I saw you without a shirt on, remember?"

Pleasure filled me at affecting him so deeply. I hadn't had much time to worry over vanity since I had moved here, but his admission made me feel beautiful. "So, you don't want our first time to be here?"

"It's not my first time," he said, the smile dropping from his face. "But it's yours. I want it to be better."

"You mean special?" My heart was expanding so fast, I'd burst.

"Yeah, Mira. You're special. And our first time is going to be important. It feels like it, right?"

Unable to speak, I nodded.

"We'll remember it for a long time, and I don't want that part of our relationship to happen too early. And I definitely don't want it to happen out in the woods on an old blanket." Caleb lifted his hands to my neck and massaged it gently. "I want to take you out. Do this right."

"Are you going to ask me on a date, Caleb McCreedy?"

"I am, but not right now."

"Why not?" I rocked against the hard seam of his pants again, and his eyes rolled closed.

He stopped my motion by gripping my waist and leveled me with a serious look. "Because right now I'm tempted to ask you out tonight so I can take you back to my place as soon as possible. It kind of defeats what I'm trying to do for us."

With an explosive sigh, I fell backward onto the blanket and stretched out, frowning at the leaves above. "Who's driving who crazy now?"

****

Caleb

The drill was a noisy, filthy, unsafe, physically draining work place. I loved it. There was no other job I wanted to do than one out on a land rig. The metal screeched around me as heavy machinery was pulled to and from the rig floor. I trusted Brian not to hit us with anything.

"Evan, cut it out," I warned as my brother sprayed Reyes with the hose like a child. There was no room for horseplay up here. A misstep didn't mean you got written up by an annoyed employer. It meant you got seriously injured—or worse.

Evan flipped me off but put the spray back on the drill as it slowly retreated out of the earth. With a clang, it pulled free, and I turned off the mud pumps. Evan and Reyes hooked the slips around the joints of the pipe, and I hopped down off my platform to help pull the length of metal upward.

"You and me, we need to switch jobs for a day," Reyes said through a muddy grin.

"I already put my time in as a floorhand. I'm good."

Reyes was an old friend who had moved off after high school. When his mother got sick about six months back, he came snooping around for a rig job, and I put in a good word. He was a greenhorn and had a lot to learn, but he would be an asset—eventually. I still watched him like a hawk, though. Evan on the floor tended to bring out everyone's worst behavior. Which was probably why, after so much time, he was still in the exact position he'd been hired in and hadn't ever seen an increase in pay. I adjusted my hard hat and booted mud off the metal decking while I waited for Reyes to clamp on the tongs before we lifted.

"Caleb," our supervisor called from above us. "Need to talk at you."

I finished hauling the pipe and glared at Evan. "You think you can add more pipe without messing up?" The slow churning fury I kept inside threatened to escape when he saluted me. Evan had only become more obnoxious with age.

I took off my work gloves and scaled the metal stairs two at a time until I reached the platform Mr. Wilson waited on. "Yes, sir?"

"Got a call from the big rig. Said they need to know your answer today. They're already working shorthanded."

I rubbed my hand over the stubble on my face. I wasn't ready to make the decision. By all accounts, I should've been. I'd known the position was mine if I wanted it since the night of the disastrous family dinner with Mira. My father had enlightened me. This was my chance. I should've jumped at it already, but I couldn't quite escape the panic that hit me in the gut when I thought about moving three hours away from home. Away from her.

"Afraid I'm going to have to respectfully decline."

Mr. Wilson stared at me like I had spoken to him in Gaelic. "I don't understand. Have you thought this through, son? I mean, ignoring the significant pay raise, you'd be on the fast track. You can't work a rig forever, McCreedy. Your body will get older and refuse you. With your knowhow, work ethic, and name? You have a chance to get in on the business side of this eventually. You won't have to be an old timer doing this kind of labor."

"I like this kind of labor, sir. My answer is no."

Mr. Wilson took his hard hat off and ran his fingers through his graying hair. He opened his mouth to object but was interrupted by a short yell and the clang of metal against metal. My legs were moving before I even fully registered the scene below me. The floor thudded as my mud-covered boots hit it running. Evan hovered over Reyes and yelled for help. Reyes held his bleeding hand to his stomach and rocked as if it would ease the pain. Open flesh hung from the side of his palm, and I cursed. It looked fucking ruined. I wanted to hit Evan. There wasn't any doubt in my mind this was his fault. I swallowed a snarl and averted my eyes in case the damned things were glowing under my fury.

"We need to get him to the clinic," I barked out.

Mr. Wilson handed me the first aid kit he'd swiped from one of the stashes. Though they tended to be well stocked and not your average medical supplies, it was still monumentally inadequate for an injury like his. I wrapped an entire roll of gauze around his hand, ignoring his screams of pain.

Mr. Wilson squatted beside me. "Evan, drive him into town," he ordered.

Evan leaned against the rail like we had offered him a rat. "Me? Why don't you make your golden boy do it?"

Mr. Wilson's face turned a deep shade of furious red. "Because that golden boy actually works around here."

Evan crossed his arms stubbornly. "No, thanks. Don't want him bleeding like a stuck pig all over my truck."

I didn't hesitate. I tossed him the keys to my truck. It wasn't surprising in the least that he worried about his trashed out pickup over his friend. That was just Evan.

He sighed heavily and stomped down the stairs, leaving Mr. Wilson and I to trail behind with a very pale looking Reyes propped between us.

****

Mira

How would I ever get used to the feel of touch? I had gone for so long without any kind of physical contact. It sent my skin buzzing. I brushed my mouth with my fingertips and imagined for the thousandth time what Caleb's soft lips had felt like against mine.

Even more important than affection, Caleb had opened up and shared his favorite spot. He'd held my hand the entire way back to the house and kissed me at the front door when he dropped me off. And he'd returned and kissed me again before he made it all the way to his truck, like he couldn't get enough. My lips throbbed just thinking about the way he'd kissed me for half an hour before he left.

"Oh, lover girl," Opal sang as she slammed the phone into its sling.

I straightened and laughed in embarrassment. I had spent most of the day in a dream. The lunch rush was over and only a few customers remained. All satisfied and not wanting for anything, I had drifted off down memory lane. Again.

"We got an order for three Very Cherry pies. They are picking them up first thing in the morning. Put the big sugar granules on top like you did last time." Her voice faded as she disappeared into the back room, but I could still hear her when she said, "They're like little tongue orgasms."

Shaking my head, I sighed. I mean really. How could a thing as small as a kiss make me feel so different? My hands went to work while my mind twirled merrily on its way.

"What do you recommend?" Caleb asked from behind me.

His voice startled me, and I let off a loud squeak. I spun around and knocked the yellow flour container to the floor. A culinary smoke cloud wafted around me like I was supposed to disappear in a magic show.

Opal poked her head out of the storage room and looked from me to Caleb and held out a broom.

Caleb leaned over the counter to better see her. "I'm sorry, Ms. Opal. That was my fault. I scared her." He was trying unsuccessfully not to smile.

"If you're here to harass my girl, you're going to have to wait until after her shift is over."

"No ma'am. I heard you guys have the best dessert around. Just got off of work and wanted to try some is all."

"Hmm," she said through narrowed eyes. The corner of her mouth was turned up in a tiny smile, though, which softened her expression. "Mira made a lemon pie this morning that is to die for." She winked. "We are calling it Grizzly Bear Meringue."

Caleb huffed a laugh. "Well, I'll have to have a slice of that one, then."

I wiped my hands on my apron and pulled a slice out of the front display case for him. My hands shook as I rang him up.

"Hey," he said, grabbing my fingers as I held out his change. "You all right?" He looked down at my hand with a worried frown.

"Yes, I'm fine," I whispered. "You just startled me."

He ran a thumb over my knuckles, leaving a trail of heat where his skin touched mine. Caleb's smile said he liked my physical reaction to him. "When do you get off?"

"Uh." I looked at the clock on the back wall. "Two more hours. Why?"

"You want to go out tonight?"

I hesitated. My heart was in my throat, and if I spoke too soon, he would be able to hear how downright giddy I felt. *Deep breath.* "Okay."

He looked surprised, but for the life of me, I couldn't figure out why. I'd basically thrown myself at him yesterday. "Yeah?" he asked.

I nodded.

"Okay. I'm going to go get ready. I'll pick you up here in two hours."

He took his pie to go and looked back at me with a grin that just about buckled my knees before he walked out the front door. If I didn't have his crumpled dollar bills in the palm of my hand, I would've sworn I'd just dreamed him.

Chapter Eighteen
Mira

It was double feature night at the drive-in movie theater, and both had been released a long time ago. This week was an alien flick followed by a romantic comedy. We showed up late, and as Caleb maneuvered his truck into one of the leftover spots in the back, I decided I was grateful we had missed most of the first one. If the ending was anything to go by, the rest of it looked terrible.

The gears clicked as Caleb shifted into park. "You want any snacks?"

My back stiffened in surprise. This was only my second time at the drive-in. The first one consisted of me sneaking around the back of the property and watching a show from behind the wire fence before Sheriff Clancy had chased me off. I had most certainly never dreamed of getting snacks. "No thank you," I said quietly. I didn't want him spending any more money on me. He had already paid for the tickets, despite my offer of part of the paycheck Opal had handed me at lunchtime.

He stared at me for a second longer. "Okay, well, I'm getting popcorn and a drink. And maybe skittles, or maybe M&M's." He ticked his future purchases off on his hand. "I won't be able to eat it all so you might as well share with me. Nachos. Do you like jalapeños?"

I sighed through a flattered smile. "Skittles and jalapeños on the side."

Caleb snaked his hand across the top of my leg and squeezed it gently. "Hey, tonight don't worry about money. Let me take you out. Okay?"

Even if I had been able to talk while swimming in the deep blue of his eyes, I definitely couldn't peep a single word with his warm, able hand across the top of my thigh. I held my breath, afraid it would match the frantic pace of my heart, and tipped my chin slightly in answer.

My gaze was drawn to his lips. They were turned up in a knowing smile. Masculine lips over a chiseled jaw. Their subtle color contrasted against the white of an alluring smile. Two faint dimples adorned his cheeks, and I was hypnotized by the ease with which he bestowed such a look on someone like me. I had never seen him give the same smile to anybody else. This one was mine.

Caleb's fingers splayed against my leg as he leaned in to kiss me. He stopped right before his lips touched mine. His smile said it wasn't a hesitation, but an invitation. I pushed a strand of blond hair out of his face with the tip of my finger and closed the small space between us. His nearness, his touch left me dizzy and needing more. He was powerful and consuming and frustrating and I wanted more like some desert animal dying of thirst. He was my sustenance.

I sucked gently on his bottom lip, and he growled softly, deep in his throat where only I would hear. I shivered at the sound. Something deep inside of me clenched at the realization that I had brought such an urgent sound from him.

Caleb pulled away, regretfully, and leaned his forehead against my own. "I think I should go get our food," he rasped.

"Sprite," I whispered, and he chuckled.

"You got it." Caleb looked at me for a moment longer before he hopped out of the truck and shut the door behind him.

I watched him move smoothly to hook the old fashioned drive-in speaker onto the open window. I had to know. "Caleb?"

"Hmm?" he asked, distracted.

"What's changed?"

He scooted the speaker over and leaned against the window. His brow furrowed as he took his time to think about his response. "I guess I just got tired of making us both miserable. I had all these reasons, but then when I looked at you, when I kissed you, I didn't really remember them anymore."

He dropped his gaze and bumped his palms against the window frame once, then strode off in the direction of a rickety concession shack to the right of the giant screen.

How was I supposed to pay attention to the movie after an admission like that? My head swam with the thought that he cared about me like this. Yesterday in the woods, he'd eased me into being comfortable and accepting my place beside him, but I'd overthought everything last night as I lay awake for hours in my bed. Shyness had crept into me again by dawn.

Caleb McCreedy, most sought after bachelor in town, was chasing me.

A little, triumphant part of me thought no one knew him quite like I did. We were scarred in different ways, but damaged just the same. He trusted me with his secret, like he knew I'd do anything to keep him and the animal that lived within him safe. I didn't have to hide from him. He'd seen me starving and weak. He'd seen my marred skin and hadn't balked against the sight. In turn, I wasn't afraid of anything he could say to me. I wanted to know everything about him. About what made him Caleb. About what made him seem so detached from every person but me. I squeezed my hands into fists to bring myself back to reality. The gesture helped me to avoid the tidal wave of emotion that threatened to overwhelm my elated heart.

I was mostly in control of myself again by the time Caleb returned with a cardboard container stacked with our sugary wares. If there had been a test at the end of the movie, I would've failed with flying colors. I couldn't focus on the plot or characters when Caleb was sitting right beside me, an arm slung over my shoulders and sharing every bit of his food with me. He laughed at the show as if we had been in the same position a hundred times. He had a deep, booming kind of laugh. I found myself wishing for more humorous lines so I could hear it again. His laughter pried some dark part of my heart open and released residual fear from the hidden crevices.

As the credits rolled, Caleb handed me the humongous drink he'd purchased and tossed our empty wrappers into the popcorn bucket. "So, I was going to take you into the city to go to a nice restaurant but we probably wouldn't get back until late. Figured I'd ask what you want to do. I have to be on the rig early in the morning, and I know you work early, too."

I looked down at my clothes. I wanted nothing more than to go to a fancy restaurant with Caleb but jeans, T-shirt, and a giant, camouflage-printed hoodie that Caleb thoughtfully gave to me weren't exactly the right attire.

"How about I take you out on Friday night?" he asked, apparently seeing my dilemma. "You can plan what you want to wear, and I'll pick you up at your house. We'll do it right."

"What is our other option for tonight?" I wasn't hungry after the pound of nachos I'd inhaled, but I wasn't ready to end the night with Caleb either.

"A romantic night at Rooney's bar."

"Perfect." I grinned, hopeful that they served pancakes in the evenings. I'd want food again eventually.

We filed out of the parking lot with the other movie goers, but Caleb hit the brakes when someone jogged up to the truck. Brian came from a raucous group who were laughing and horsing around a trio of closely parked jeeps.

He waved and beamed when he saw me. "Hey, Mira. You guys on a date or something?"

I froze. Caleb did not. "Yep," he said, void of hesitation. "About to take her to Rooney's."

Brian snorted and jutted a thumb at Caleb. "You sure you want to go out with a guy who takes you to a bar for your first date?"

I was so relieved he wasn't treating me like a pariah that I found my voice. "Technically, this is our second date."

Caleb looked at me questioningly. A confused smile lingered on his lips.

"He took me for breakfast a while back," I explained.

"Oh, yeah?" Brian asked. "Where?"

"The bar," I said through a smirk.

The brothers barked laughter, and Brian shook his head in mock disappointment. "All right, Romeo, we'll be at the old McCall farm if you guys get bored. Booze, a field, cows to tip. Should be a good time." He turned to leave. "Make good decisions," he called over his shoulder.

"That's the first party I have ever been invited to," I admitted out loud.

Caleb draped his arm over the steering wheel like he was in no hurry to leave. "We can go if you want to."

"Do you want to go?" I asked.

"Not really my scene. More than likely, there will be a lot of people there."

"Okay good, because that sounds terrifying."

Caleb waved to a couple of hecklers sitting on top of the hood of the darkest colored jeep who made kissing sounds in our direction. A smile still lingered on his lips as he pulled out of the parking lot.

Rooney's Bar was quiet with only a few older men sitting at the bar. A couple of tables were occupied, but the booth in the corner was wide open and beckoning us. It was also the farthest point from the pungent veil of smoke that hung over the bar top.

"What made you decide to work on the rig?" I asked as the waitress put two sweet teas on the table between us.

Caleb rubbed the knuckle on my hand thoughtfully and leaned back. "At first I wanted to work it because of my dad. I wanted to make him proud. But eventually, I figured out that I really liked it. I like the challenge. I like learning the different jobs on it. I work well under pressure and with deadlines. I even like the crazy shifts." He shrugged self-deprecatingly. "Can't imagine working a different job."

"Is it dangerous?"

Caleb smiled mischievously. "Why, you worried about me?"

My poker face was pitiful thanks to minimal contact with other humans. Unfortunate. Caleb's grin only grew wider, so primly, I said, "I'm sure you're completely capable of handling yourself at your job." I took a long, sobering draw of tea from the straw. "You didn't answer my question."

"Yes, it is. But that's included in the challenge part that I love so much."

He liked his job. I'd worry in silence and spare him my concern.

Achy Breaky Heart blared out of the dusty, old jukebox in the corner. I groaned internally but Caleb grabbed my hand. "Come on," he said.

We took our time choosing the perfect song. He fed the machine a quarter and I pressed J-14. Tom Petty and the Heartbreakers sang to the uninterested bar about how waiting was the hardest part.

"Burgers are ready," the waitress called.

Caleb waved and led me back to our booth. He waited until I was seated to take his own. I thought it sweet that, for all his rough edges, he still had the manners that were probably expected in our grandfathers' day.

"You ever had a boyfriend?" Caleb asked. His cheeks flushed and the mortified look on his face told me he didn't mean to wonder out loud.

My face was probably scarlet, too. I tried to ease his discomfort by answering. "Once. I was twelve."

Caleb's eyes danced with relief. "What was his name?"

"Jeremiah Prichard. He was short and brainy, but he didn't ask me too many questions, and he talked enough for the both of us. I let him hold my hand once."

Caleb passed me an onion ring off his plate. "Scandalous."

"I thought so. My foster parents would have whipped me good if they found out. That particular couple had a distinct paranoia about their foster kids getting knocked up on their watch." I giggled at the memory as I shoveled a forkful of cheese fries onto Caleb's plate, but he stared at me with ghosts in his eyes.

"Do you ever wish things would've been different?" he asked.

I shrugged as if it would lift the unease at dredging up old memories. "No use crying over spilt milk. I'll be right back," I said, excusing myself. The gritty bits and stories from my past left me raw and exposed, and I didn't want to ruin the night with them. I needed a minute to put the screaming demons back in their boxes before they came tumbling out for all to see.

The bathroom mirror was a judgmental little beast. As I stared at my pale face, I could all but hear the *scritch scratch* of little claws tearing at my chain-locked memories. Things I had long ago put away for a day when I was strong enough to deal with them. The locks rattled, thunking softly against memories of my whiskey-shootin' stepdad, and I took a deep breath to steady myself. Thinking about him now would undo me. Maybe I really was crazy like everyone said.

Caleb deserved better. I didn't disagree, but I could sure as hell justify going straight back to that table and trying to be better for him.

Rooney's had changed during my short-lived escape. Minutes ago, it had been a barren landscape with only a few men drinking or snoring softly against the bar top. Now, it was another planet entirely. Every square foot of space was taken by a body. The air stank of cigarette smoke and grease. My gaze fell on Caleb, like a paperclip to a magnet. He sat at our booth, and through the gyrating, raucous crowd, I could see that our table was now full. Becca plucked a fry unapologetically from my plate.

I hesitated. A slow fury burned in me, and I couldn't bear down on them in such a state. They would see me as a starving dog defending a meal. Caleb scanned the crowd and lit up with obvious relief when he saw me. The crowd pulsed as we tried to reach each other. Everyone was lost in their own world, dancing to a rhythm that was more internal than to the barely audible jukebox music. I laughed at the ridiculousness of our effort as Caleb reached me. I didn't know if it was the energy from the crowd or his frustration over Becca, but his lips crashed down on mine.

I was shocked into stillness, but as the masses around us kept dancing, I gave into him. I was reckless to be closer to him. I splayed my fingers against the expanse of his chest and felt the hard planes there through the thin cotton of his shirt. A delicious desperation fed his kiss. I touched the long scars that ran down his neck, and he shuddered and dragged my waist closer to him. I wasn't concerned with hurting his healing wounds. I wanted him to feel me. My mind had stayed stubbornly on those beautiful marks across his flesh for weeks, and I couldn't wait any longer to feel them beneath my touch. "Caleb," I said, raggedly. I would lose my mind if he didn't stop.

He pulled away, panting. "Dance with me."

It was a natural transition from touching him to dancing with him. I had never danced with a man before, but my body didn't seem to care.

I wondered where my shyness had gone as I moved and laughed and spun. Caleb didn't take his eyes off me, and when the song was through, we giggled our way off the dance floor.

"Caleb! Mira!" someone yelled over the crowd.

I turned to see Brian waving us back to the table. Tempting if Evan weren't there watching me like a tiger watches a mouse, and if Becca wasn't shooting me with flaming death daggers from her eyes. I shook my head at Caleb's questioning look and waved to his brother before I darted out the front door. Caleb paid for our meal and joined me a few minutes later.

My blood hummed with the high of dancing with Caleb, and I couldn't quite stop myself from smiling. His hand was warm and strong in mine as he led me to his truck, and an unfamiliar warmth spread to unknown depths inside of me. We dodged comers and goers, and Caleb jerked the tailgate of his truck down and set me easily upon it. I leaned back on locked elbows, the palms of my hands griping at the contrast between the cold metal and Caleb's absent warmth.

He put his hips between my knees and talked easily. "Sorry about the crowd. Apparently somebody called Sheriff Clancy and warned him about the party going down at the McCall farm. Brian thinks it was Becca who blew the whistle. So, they peeled out as soon as they saw the flashing lights and moved the party to Rooney's."

"I don't mind," I said quietly, my shyness returning little by little. "It was actually kind of fun."

"Yeah?" He donned a slow smile. "For me, too."

The moon sat full and low in the sky, and I scrunched my nose. "It's getting late."

"Yeah, I'd better get you home." He helped me down from the tailgate and closed it while I scrambled into the cab of his truck.

The remnants of recklessness clung to me as he pulled into first gear. Desperate to cast away the creeping shyness that seemed determined to overshadow the remaining high from dancing, I slid over the bench seat and pressed into his side. He tossed me a quick smile that said he liked me this close and pulled out of the lot. At the one stoplight in town, he leaned over and kissed my temple, and I rested my head on his shoulder. The radio played a soft country song, and Caleb's fingertips stroked the palm of my hand until my heart raced. My traitorous knees opened for him, and his eyes churned as he watched their movement. He ran a light touch up the inside of my knee, and I closed my eyes against the shiver that shook my spine and shoulders.

When I opened them again, the light was yellow and we'd definitely missed our chance to go. No one was behind us, though, so it was really hard to care. Caleb's mouth covered mine, and my cheek caught fire where the pad of his thumb rested. Parting my lips, I tasted him and ran my fingers down his stomach. I wanted to feel all of him. His breathing became ragged as he dragged me closer still. The red glow changed to green against his cheeks as the light turned, and he hit the gas and pulled away as I ran kisses down his neck. His breath came unsteady, and a fierce look of concentration took his face as he stared at the road in front of us. His mind was on me, though. I knew it with certainty. I ran my hand down the length of his erection, rock hard under the tight fabric of his jeans.

"Dammit, woman. You have to stop." His voice was rough like gravel, and he bucked against my hand.

This was too fun to stop. His knuckles shone white against the steering wheel. A muscle ticked under his right eye, and his neck strained with every stroke. He made it all the way up Dark Corner, past my gate, and into the woods before he slammed the truck into park and cut the lights.

I was on fire, burning from within, and the only thing that would save me was his skin against mine.

I loved him. I *loved* him. I adored every single thing about him.

"Mira," Caleb growled. "You're making it really hard to be a gentleman."

Gentle sounded overrated. "Caleb," I breathed, laying back on the bench seat, "I already know you're a good man, but so does everyone else. I want more. I want to know all of you."

My mind was gone. All logic had fled me at the stoplight, and now the only thing that would satiate me was Caleb's to give. His eyes never left mine as he rose above me and lowered himself against my hips. He was big, strong, and captivating, and just when I thought I would suffocate under his power, he reached back and shoved the driver's side door open. Cool air assaulted us, and I gasped as he rubbed against my pelvis. A desperate sound clawed its way up the back of my throat as I fumbled with the button on my jeans.

"Stop," Caleb said.

"But—"

He shook his head, cutting off my complaints. "We've got time." His able fingers plucked the button where I'd failed, and the slow rip of my zipper filled the cab. He peeled my jeans from me, but the red, lacy underwear I'd picked up from Bealls last week stayed irritatingly on my hips. He studied my pout, and a smirk took his lips. "I told you the first time would be special, Mira." He made a show of looking around, one golden eyebrow winged up. "This ain't it."

"Damn you, Caleb." My voice had dropped to a whisper, and I crossed my arms over my chest like a shield. "I feel like I'm falling apart."

He leaned down with a smirk, and his kiss was slow, languid, and teasing. I wanted to bite him. After he moved his hips to the side, the lightest brush of his fingers trailed up the inside of my bare thigh. Nuzzling my neck, he murmured, "Don't damn me, woman. I haven't let you fall apart yet."

Cool air hit my moist skin as Caleb pulled my panties to the side. He blocked the breeze by cupping my sex, and I gasped at the feel of his hand against me. As I drew my knee up, I uttered, "Please."

His lips moved against my throat, and he rubbed torturous circles against me with the softest touch. The man was going to make me beg, and sadly, I wasn't above it. And just as I opened my mouth to plead, he slid a slow finger inside of me, drawing a shudder from me as I bore down. The moan that came from my throat overshadowed the cicadas and crickets of the night woods. Frantic for more, I slid my hand over his and pulled him into me again.

The shake of his head was unrushed. "No." Prying my palm away, he pushed it above my head with his free hand and held it there. "Tonight you're mine, and I'll go as slow as I like."

He pressed into me again, and I trembled, desperate for more. Long, languid strokes built pressure I was insane to banish, but still, he held me there, just on the edge. I pulled my hand from his wrist and clenched his shirt, arched back against him until my stomach brushed the fabric of his black, thermal sweater. Caleb hunched in on himself at my touch, letting me see that he wasn't as in control as he played at. He was hanging by a thread, too, and when he dragged his hungry, inhuman gaze back to mine, I whispered, "I like you."

Oh, he knew what I meant, and his eyes turned to blazing gold flames. Cursing, he bucked against my hip and dropped his head until his teeth grazed my shoulder. I rocked, and he let me set the pace now. Clutching onto him, digging my nails into his skin through his shirt, three more fast strokes and I shattered, yelling his name as he pressed into me and held.

His chest heaved as he squeezed his eyes closed against whatever urges he was fighting, and it all became so clear.

He said I was his tonight, but now, he was also mine, too.

****

I thought it was Caleb who knocked on my door after our night was through. Who else would be at my place at such an hour? Who else was brave enough to travel my haunted woods at night? He must have forgotten something. His hoodie still clung intimately to my torso, and he probably needed it back. I hummed as I made my way to the door, but my old mangy dog, Brady, growled out his warning just as I reached for the handle. Too late.

"Evenin', Mira," Evan drawled as he leaned against the frame of my doorway.

"No," I said, as if he'd asked a question. "You are not invited in."

"I'm not a vampire, Mira," Evan said, shoving his way past me. "That shit doesn't work on me."

I scuttled behind the kitchen table and held onto a chair with a steely grip, as if doing so would give me the strength I needed to throw it at Evan if I felt so inclined.

"What are you doing here?" I demanded.

"Pipe down, Crazy Mira. I'm not going to murder you or anything. I came to pass along a little information, is all."

He leaned across the table, and I backed up, the chair in my hands shuffling loudly against the grain of the wooden floors as I dragged it with me.

"Look, I came here to tell you, you should forget about my brother. Just let him alone."

"Why would I do that?" I asked shakily.

"Because from the way you look at him, I can tell you care about him. And if you care about him like I think you do, you won't hold him back."

I stared at him, completely at a loss to what he was going on about. He may as well have been speaking in pig latin, which I didn't happen to know the formula for.

Evan growled with impatience. "Look, you crazy skank. If you know anything at all about my brother, you know his job is his life. And he just turned down the chance of a lifetime to work on a big rig as a supervisor because he's all hung up on staying close to you. He would be the youngest man at that position for fuck's sake. And that idiot turned it down flat. Your fault, Mira. Fix it." Evan turned and left the house without another word.

I closed my mouth and wondered abstractedly if it had been hanging open the entire time Evan had lectured me.

"I'm not a crazy skank," I grumbled as I slunk down into the chair I had used as a barrier the moment before.

Evan's motivation for bestowing such information on me was unimportant. I didn't have any doubts that it was for some dark reason, but if what he said was true, I couldn't let Caleb give up his dreams for me. He had a future. An important one. He was going somewhere while the rest of this sleepy town was frozen in place. I couldn't rob him of that.

The selfish parts of me argued. He had made his choice. He had come after me. He had scaled that wall at the parade and invited everyone to watch him choose me. I could keep him.

Damn Evan for not telling me at Rooney's before I gave my heart completely to Caleb in the front seat of his Ford. In a wave of fury, I picked up the ceramic vase that sat idly on the table and threw it against the wall with a tremendous crash. I screamed and put my head in my hands. Why? Why couldn't I, for once in my entire, miserable existence, have something that made me feel happy? That made me feel safe?

I wouldn't be able to live with myself, knowing every day I took something from him—something so vital to his happiness. I wanted to give him things, not take them away.

I would never want anyone else. I had chosen to give my heart to the only man it found worthy, and now I would have to rip it away from his protective grasp. It was too late. The damage had been done.

His lips against mine, his secret smile, our dance, his touch. It would have to be enough to last my entire life.

Chapter Nineteen
Caleb

I spent more time than I thought possible picking out flowers for Mira. The tiny florist off Main Street didn't have that big of a selection, and still I stood staring at the bouquets for twenty minutes, at least.

I hopped out of the truck and opened the gate to Mira's property, mindful of stepping around a gigantic pile of horse crap so I didn't get my dress shoes dirty. The windows were down and the crisp autumn air bit into my flesh. I ignored it and turned up the radio. Open windows made Mira more comfortable and relaxed my inner animal, so down they'd stay.

The truck bounced along for what seemed like forever in my haste to see Mira again. I hadn't been able to keep my mind off her after our date. The rig kept me busy, but she wasn't far from my thoughts. I couldn't stop thinking about the way she'd looked when we danced, or when she was reclined in the bed of my truck, smiling at me like I was the most important man in the world. Or the way she said my name when I touched her. That little moment visited my memories whenever I sat behind the wheel. She was perfect.

My knuckles made a hollow sound as they rapped against her front door. It was as if they already knew she wasn't inside. I slid a glance to my watch. *Right on time.* I squinted at the door, then hopped off the porch.

I opened my senses, something I was learning to hone more and more. The subtle sound of human movement touched my ears, and I headed around the corner, flowers in hand. I opened my mouth to call out to her, but stopped when I saw what she was doing.

Hunting season was the same every year. October and November came, and droves of hunters descended upon the open forest around here. In every bar and restaurant and gas station, you could find men and women dressed in camouflage with sheathed hunting knives hanging from their waists.

Mira, apparently, was one of them.

She had a wild hog hanging from a tree upside down from a pulley system. She jerked and cut with the easy precision of someone who had harvested game a hundred times. Her arms were covered in blood up to her elbows, and her face was frozen in the fierce concentration of a woman who knew exactly how sharp her knife was.

I was at once startled and intrigued. Three more swift cuts and the back strap came free. She tossed it into a black plastic bag and went back to work without so much as wiping sweat from her brow. Her quiet turmoil confused me. I sat slowly on the middle step of her back porch and watched her work, as if doing so would help me to solve the mystery of which inner demon was eating her alive right now. I would have to cancel our reservation in the city.

She had to have known I was here. She was as skittish as a half-broke pony. Her senses wouldn't have missed me sitting so close.

She moved around the hog to remove the tenderloins, and the half-harvested animal sagged as the pulley system failed.

Mira cursed under her breath and shoved her knife dexterously into the sheath that peeked out of her pocket. She caught the rope, but I was already headed toward her to help.

"Don't," she yelled, failing to meet my eyes.

I froze, my hands out as if they still wanted something to do.

Mira yanked violently on the pulley and tied the end of the rope more securely around the trunk of the tree. "I don't need your help." Her voice shook.

I was at a loss. I opened my mouth but only an inaudible sound of confusion came out.

Mira wiped her face against her shoulder and waited, eyes on the ground.

"What did I do?" I asked, putting a voice to my confusion.

"Nothing. You didn't do anything wrong. I just—" Mira bit her bottom lip, but not before I saw the tremble there.

I lowered my voice. "Why don't we just go get cleaned up and go on our date, and we can talk about whatever is bothering you. We'll fix it."

"It can't be fixed. Don't you get it? *I* can't be fixed."

"No, I don't get it, Mira. I have no idea what I have done to piss you off, and you're talking in riddles. Just tell me what you want from me."

"I don't want anything from you. You pushed me to get a job. You fixed my whole damned house to look like it belongs in some Pottery Barn catalog. You force me to spend time in town with all of the people who have hurt me. I was happy, Caleb. Before you came along, I was hungry, sure, but I knew my place in the world. I'm not good enough for you if you don't turn me into a proper townie, and I don't want it. I don't want any of it. I don't think I should go on a date with you."

I shook my head slowly back and forth. "Why are you acting like this?"

"Like what? Like I'm crazy? Because I am. You've just been too dumb or too stubborn to see it. Every single person in town knows it, Caleb. Time you accept it, too. Please leave."

I clenched my jaw to stop from yelling. Didn't she see? I couldn't just leave and forget about her. She had changed me—permanently. "I'll give you space," I gritted out. "We'll talk about this in a few days when you aren't so angry. It can't just end like this, though. I need more."

Mira looked like she was going to be sick. She was pale, and her hands shook. She swayed slightly when she uttered the words, "That's the problem. You need me, but I don't need you."

And just like that, I knew she was right. I had suspected it since the day she had stitched up the damage Eli had done to me. She didn't need a man to complete her, to walk side-by-side with her. She was as lonely as the long whistle of a midnight train, but that's how she preferred it. The realization cut me deeper than that bear shifter ever could have. I knew I needed her. I hadn't needed anyone since Mom died, and in desperation to connect with Mira, I had given in. And that was proving to be the biggest mistake of my life because I had allowed in a pain so acute, I would drown in it.

Without another word I left, fists clenched and a sea of red threatening to overwhelm me. My ears roared as I jerked open the door to my truck and sat in the front seat, wanting nothing more than to scream until I couldn't see straight.

I left Mira to her beloved, lonely existence.

****

Mira

The door to Caleb's truck slammed shut, and he peeled out of my front yard. I squatted down and pulled my hands over my head as if that would keep all of my shattering pieces together. My fingers wound painfully in my hair as I clenched my tresses, and a sob escaped my lips. How would I ever recover from something so painful? I hadn't meant any of it. Not a bit. I was grateful to Caleb for giving me a life. For giving me a future with all the basic necessities so many took for granted. I was thankful for the change he had started in me. He had never tried to transform me to fit what he wanted in a woman. I just didn't know what else to say to get him to move on.

He'd take the job on the big rig. Meet a nice, normal girl and live in a big house. I would always respect what I had done, setting him free like that, but hate myself, too. No one would suffer more than me.

And telling him, so cruelly, that I didn't need him like he needed me...

I wretched. In one fluid motion, I stood and pulled the knife from its leather case in my pocket. I hurled it at a nearby tree. It spun in a beautiful dance before it shanked off my intended target and ricocheted off into the woods. I turned away from my failure to find a dash of color sitting forlornly on the porch.

My breath hitched in misery as I touched the edge of a pink rose with the tip of my finger. He'd brought me flowers. I clutched them to my chest with bloody hands and cried on the stairs until my head ached from the emotional effort.

Hours stretched into night and day again. Evenings were the loneliest when I had nothing to do but think about Caleb. My tears washed away the things I'd begun to like about myself.

Later that week, Brian came by the pie shop and kindly told me that Caleb had, in fact, accepted the job on the big rig three hours away. And though it had been my plan to give him the life he deserved, the realization that Caleb was really lost to me was a new and devastating cut.

I worked for Opal in a numb haze. My hands did their job, but my mind, in an effort to protect itself from the hurt, bumbled from one unimportant thought to the next, the background noise nothing more than the sound of a beehive in late spring.

I'd had him. For one bright and explosive moment, I had everything. A future and a man who loved me. Safety. It would have been better if I'd never had anything at all. If I could erase it, I would. I'd have gone back to existing instead of living if it meant the clenching, suffocating tightness inside my chest would ease.

****

Caleb

Becca hailed me from across the street, but I did my best to ignore her. Maybe if she thought I didn't see her, she would give up on whatever annoying errand she was on. Apparently, I gave her way too much credit.

"Caleb," she shouted, stopping just about everyone on Main Street. I growled and turned to glare at her. "What do you want, Becca?"

She jogged across the street with a large stack of papers in her hands. "I just thought you would want to know some things about your little girlfriend before they become public knowledge."

"We're not together anymore." I walked off but Becca followed closely behind.

"Well, thank goodness you finally came to your senses because, apparently, Crazy Mira really is crazy."

I sighed in utter irritation and rounded on her. "What are you talking about?"

Becca shoved a stapled stack of papers into my chest. "Mira spent a year in a mental institution. Says so right there in her report, along with a whole list of things she was admitted for."

"What? Where did you get this?" I asked.

"That doesn't matter, Caleb. You're completely missing the point."

I narrowed my eyes at her. "Tell me Sheriff Clancy doesn't know about you getting these."

Becca straightened her spine and lifted her chin primly. "He doesn't."

I wanted to laugh at her gall. It was an insult to her character that I wasn't even surprised. I snatched the stack of papers she still clung to and marched toward my truck.

"I still have the original," Becca sang after me. "I can always make more copies."

I tried to make it all the way home before I read Mira's records, but I couldn't. The truck skidded to a stop on the side of the road, and I pinned the first page against the steering wheel.

Post-Traumatic Stress Syndrome
Depression
Possible Bipolar Disorder
Speech Impediments due to Mental Trauma
Violent Outbursts
Panic Attacks
Chronic Anxiety

The list went on to name the medications they had tried on her. Which ones worked and which ones didn't. Sedatives seemed to be the only thing that helped consistently.

I did some quick math on the date. Mira had been ten years old at the time. A part of me wanted to mourn for what she'd been through, and another part was pissed that she never told me anything about such a huge childhood experience. I flipped through a small rap sheet, mostly made up of Sheriff Clancy's disturbing-the-peace arrests, then leaned back into the seat.

I really didn't know Mira at all.

Chapter Twenty
Mira

"I'm taking a break," I informed Opal, who sat comfortably on the stepstool in the storage room, taking inventory. "Keep an eye on the front?"

"Yeah, yeah. You got it. See you in fifteen," she said in a distracted voice.

Her pen tapped loudly against her clipboard, and I knew she was doing math. "It helps me focus," she had told me one day when I couldn't stop staring at her pen, blurred with motion.

I had big plans to run down to the gas station and buy a two pack of Twinkies as a reward for surviving the past week. Never before had I tasted one, but I'd heard good things, and I needed a distraction. The corner of a piece of paper taped to the door lifted and fluttered in the breeze. Opal didn't normally allow flyers on her windows so, out of curiosity, I stopped to read it.

The sound of my heart was deafening as I read the dreaded summary of my past. I gasped as I ripped it off the window and glanced around to see if anyone else had read it. Clusters of people talked in hushed whispers as they watched me, and my gaze crashed into a telephone pole that held another report. Proof of my mental instability.

Copies were attached to every visible wooden or glass surface on Main Street, like a snowstorm of my indiscretions. Horror sat on my chest and made it hard to breathe. "No, no, no," I chanted as I ripped page after page down and wadded them up.

"What's going on here?" Opal asked as she came out of the pie shop. She cast a confused look to the people in her store who stared out of the clear glass, like window pups at a pet store.

"Opal," I sobbed. Tears burned my eyes and trailed down my cheeks.

My fists were full of the crumpled, damning papers. Opal pulled one off a blue metal mailbox in front of her shop. She scanned it, and her face fell. "You people should be ashamed of yourselves," she yelled. Quietly, to me, she said, "Mira, go home."

I panicked. Everyone would see them. *He* would see them. "But—"

"I'll clean all of this up. You go on home now, you hear?" She turned to the gathering crowd. "Pie shop's closed for the rest of the day."

Opal turned to pull another report off the window of the shop next door. A few of the onlookers began to help her, and I bolted for my truck.

Caleb was on the rig all day. Opal would have them all cleaned up by the time he got off work. He would probably never see them. Oh, who was I kidding? Nobody took a shit in this town without every last person knowing about it.

I slammed my palm against the steering wheel, over and over until it throbbed. Who would do such a thing? Clancy and his deputy were the only ones in town who had access. What could I have possibly done to piss them off so badly that they would ruin my life like this?

I never checked my mail. It was pointless when you had lived off the grid for so long and didn't get bills. And to be perfectly honest, it wasn't like I was in danger of receiving a Christmas card. But a copy of my report fluttered in the wind, held onto the rusty old mailbox by a thin piece of tape. I threw my truck into park and jumped out to rip it off, like the faster I did, the less it would be true. The lid clunked open and a very official looking packet lay folded inside. After I wrestled it out, I read the return address logo.

Avery and Woods Law Group. The name pulled on the edges of my frayed mind. I wiped my damp lashes with the back of my hand and tossed it into the passenger seat before I got in my truck. As I drove through the woods that led home, my gaze was attracted time and time again to the oversized envelope. The only lawyer I knew was Sam Burns.

And the lawyers from the trial.

I slammed on the breaks and stared in fear at the package. My fingers couldn't work fast enough as I tore through the top and pulled the papers out. Scanning the document, my heart fell to somewhere between the soles of my feet and the rusted out floorboard.

...Angus French......released early......parole......good behavior...

The rest of the letter didn't matter to me. I was supposed to have three more years of safety, but my stepfather somehow convinced a panel he wasn't evil anymore and got himself released.

He'd be coming for me.

I scanned the date at the top and cursed myself for not checking my mail more often. He could be to my house as early as tomorrow if he got lucky with a ride. Maybe even today. My fingers clenched the paper as I searched the woods. My forest suddenly became darker, more sinister. A chill ran up my spine and gooseflesh raised over my arms as I imagined Angus watching me from some unknown hiding place in the shadows. I couldn't stay here. The Fletcher house was where he would come first.

The mouse in me said I was going to die just like Angus had told me all those years ago, but the survivor in me was already searching for a hidey hole. I needed to find asylum.

I pulled the truck around and headed for town again, my earlier dilemma forgotten in the wake of unmitigated fear. I could go to Sheriff Clancy. He was a cop. He was supposed to, by profession, help people who were in danger, right? I growled. Clancy hated me. He'd probably assist my stepdad and then dance on my grave.

Sam Burns? He was a lawyer who could get me in touch with people. Maybe he could get me into some program where they would give me a secret identity and I could hide in some foreign country for the rest of my life. I thought about my timeline and clenched my teeth together. Sam Burns didn't know anything about my case, and I didn't have time to catch him up. I had succeeded in convincing exactly zero people to believe me about my stepfather when he'd killed my mom. I doubted heavily that Sam Burns would be my first.

My truck blew through town before I even fully registered where I intended to go. In quiet desperation, I sought the only safety I'd ever known.

****

Caleb

One week. I had one more week before I'd be working on the big rig and out of this tired little town. I liked my home, but being so close to Mira was suffocating me. I didn't have it in me to watch her move on.

"Ho!" Brian yelled over the clanking machinery below.

I dragged my thoughts back to the present and set my clipboard down. Sparing a testy glare for my brother, I yelled, "What?"

Brian jerked his head toward the parking lot. "Visitor," he clipped out before he turned to help haul up another length of pipe.

I had received a visitor exactly one time at work, and that had been the day my mother passed.

I squinted down the stairs but couldn't see past the gleaming metal of the machinery that ran the rig.

"No personal shit at work, McCreedy," Mr. Wilson warned around a toothpick that hung precariously out of the corner of his downturned mouth.

"Yep. Two minutes." I handed him the clipboard and ducked down the stairs that led to the parking lot.

I spotted her green truck first, and my pulse picked up. I was mad at her but couldn't seem to tell that to my heart. It stuttered at the prospect of seeing her. She fidgeted at the bottom of the stairs, her eyes dashing around with all of the paranoia of a frightened animal.

"Why are you here?" I asked before she had even seen me.

Mira jumped, every muscle in her body seeming to spasm with the start. "Caleb," she breathed.

I didn't answer. She'd gutted me, ripped me in two, and now she was here to what? Finish me off? I crossed my arms and waited.

"Okay," she said. "Okay, I know I'm the last person you want to see right now but I need help, and I don't know who else to ask." The words tumbled from her lips like a boulder gaining momentum down the side of a towering mountain.

I grabbed her arm and pulled her toward her truck, away from the noise of the rig. Something had frightened Mira, and a lump settled in my gut. She wouldn't admit to needing my help if it wasn't something urgent. Her fear stirred up a really bad feeling and kicked up my animal. I hadn't changed in a week, trying to avoid the urge to hunt for her like I always did, but this was about to send me over the edge. "What happened?"

She took a deep, steadying breath, but a sob broke out of her. "He's out. I got home and found a letter from the lawyers in my mailbox, and now he's going to come get me. He's going to kill me!"

Nothing she said made sense. "Who's going to kill you?"

"My stepdad. Angus French."

I opened my mouth to speak but an ear-splitting whistle interrupted me. It was Evan, waving with annoyed gestures for me to get back to work. I sighed heavily. "Look, I can't do this right now. I have three more hours until my shift is done."

"You don't believe me," she said, with the most hurt expression I'd ever seen on another human being. She whirled around and jerked open the door of her truck to escape me.

I caught the door before it opened halfway and gripped the frame until my knuckles hurt from the strain. "Didn't say I don't believe you, Mira. Just that I can't deal with this until after I get off. Somebody could get hurt up there if we're shorthanded. Pull your truck up closer to the rig. Lock the doors and wait for me. You see so much as a horned toad move, you flag someone down."

Her face was so open. I could see every emotion in her eyes and, dammit, I wanted to hug her tight and reassure her I'd die before I let anything happen to her.

"We'll talk about this when I'm done." I turned to leave but the flash of fear in her eyes tore at everything in me and made me stop. "I won't let anyone hurt you."

Mira let out a long, shaky breath and the corner of her mouth turned up in the barest ghost of a smile. "I know."

How was I supposed to work after that? Any effort to stay in the here and now was thwarted by thoughts of Mira. Of the way her lips looked when she admitted she needed me. Of the way the wind lifted her hair as it brushed across her back, the dusty southern sky a backdrop to her silhouette.

And then there were the three thousand questions running through my mind about the utterly disturbing information she had given me that threatened to shut down all of my mental facilities. Every instinct in my body screamed to protect her. Even the short physical distance away from her felt like a canyon.

Three hours stretched on forever.

When at last the end of the shift came, I jogged to her truck and pulled the door closed behind me with more force than I'd intended. All of the pent up agitation somehow escaped through my fingertips. Mira didn't jump this time, like she expected no less of me.

I gripped the steering wheel. "I think you need to start by telling me where you got those scars around your neck."

"Caleb, I'm sorry." She looked at me with those dove gray eyes, begging forgiveness. "Evan came over after our date. He told me about the job offer on the big rig."

I jerked my head in surprise. Speaking of the devil himself, Evan jumped in front of the parked truck and pelvic thrusted in a circular motion with his tongue wagging. I could only imagine what he'd said to her. The urge to peel out and flip him over the hood was massive.

"Were you trying to let me go?" I asked, dragging my gaze away from my idiot brother.

A nod and a whisper. "I don't want to hold you back."

And just like that, a weight lifted from me that left me relieved and exhausted all at once. "Dammit, Mira. You won't hold me back. I can't remember being happier than when I thought you were mine. That job won't bring me peace. I like it here. I fit here." I took her hand in mine to show her the truth to my words. "Don't do that to me again. I know you meant well, but you're just going to have to trust me to make my own decisions about this stuff, okay?"

Moisture brushed her dark eyelashes but no tears fell. She smiled and squeezed my hand gently in her own. Thickly, she said, "Okay."

"The scars," I reminded her.

She sighed. "Drive. I can't do this if you're looking at me."

I spared a glance for my truck but decided it would be fine parked here until my shift in the morning. The old Chevy's idling engine sounded like a freight train, and we ambled out of the parking lot behind the rest of the crew. "Where to?"

Mira shrugged miserably. "Anywhere but home. He'll find me there." She drew her knees up to her chest as if it would protect her from the words she would say. "My stepfather, Angus, was a cruel man. He hurt my mother, and when I tried to defend her, he hurt me. One day, right after my seventh birthday party, Angus decided he fancied me."

She spared a frightened glance for me, but I tried to keep my disgust hidden behind a stoic face. If he was alive like she said, I already wanted to kill him.

"He never touched me, Caleb. I fought him, and he didn't push too hard. It was a game to him. He knew it made me uncomfortable, so it was his way of toying with me. Of hurting my mom. One night, he got really drunk and found me hiding under my bed. He said, 'Mira, you're a pretty girl, and pretty girls should have pretty things. Like a pearl necklace.' And then he took his cigarette and held me down and burned the first notch into my collar bone. And over the next year, he did the rest. He finished the necklace the night he killed my mother."

Unable to take anymore, I swore under my breath. My stomach twisted with a nauseous clenching and, for a split second, I thought I would be sick right there on the dashboard of her truck. This was the first time I realized evil really existed. "Was that when you went into the institution?"

Mira was quiet for a long time. She looked out the window and bit the end of her thumbnail. "You read my report?"

"Becca brought it to me. You could've told me, you know," I said, turning onto Dark Corner Road.

"I said we can't go to my place," she protested, straightening up with a panicked look.

"We aren't. I'm taking you to my place."

"Oh. So, Becca was the one who posted those flyers all over town?"

A fury I hadn't known before burned in my gut. I knew that girl would make copies and possibly blackmail Mira. I hadn't, however, thought she had it in her to go as far as peppering the town with that shit. "I didn't know she did that," I gritted out. "Where has Angus been all these years?"

Mira swallowed audibly. "In prison. For child abuse and child endangerment, not for murder."

"How did he get away with killing your mom?"

"Angus had planned my mother's murder down to the tiniest detail. I didn't understand that because I was only eight at the time, but he had everything nailed down to look like self-defense. The blood spatter, the trajectory and timing of the bullets. He shot himself twice, then killed her with a smile on his face. The neighbors called in the gunshots but their report matched Angus's lies. He had very good lawyers, and after what I'd seen, I had trouble speaking. I had so many thoughts and visions, memories rattling around my head that I couldn't say what I wanted to." Mira glared at the turnoff to her house as we passed. "Before the cops showed up, Angus repeated this made-up story of what happened over and over to me, but I knew what I'd seen. Because of the stutters in my story, and my trouble speaking coherently, I was deemed an unreliable witness. Angus couldn't deny the allegations that I had been abused, though. The evidence was there, still bleeding on my neck, which was exactly what he wanted the cops who arrested him to think. My mother had gone after him because he hurt me. He wanted them to think she shot him, and then he killed her in self-defense. So he got prison, but not for long enough." Having unloaded something so cavernous and dark that she had likely kept to herself for so many years, she let out a long, shaky breath. "So that's me. Crazy Mira."

I pulled the truck to a stop in front of my house. "Don't say that. You aren't crazy." I pulled her to me and hugged her tightly. "You're strong. You went through something no one should ever go through, and you survived. Screw anyone who calls you that. They don't know anything important about you. Not like I do."

Chapter Twenty-One
Mira

Maybe it would work. Maybe Angus would look and eventually give up when he couldn't find me. A knowing part of me scoffed at my naiveté. Angus was a thoughtful and organized hunter. He wouldn't give up until his heart stopped beating.

Caleb's house wasn't what I expected, which somehow made me care about him more. He didn't reside in some country mansion like the one he'd grown up in. He had spent his hard earned money on the acreage that made up his property and put a double-wide mobile home directly in the center of a meadow. The home looked new, and well-made, but when I had cause to think about where he lived, I had always imagined a large homemade of sticks and bricks.

He came around the front of the Ford and opened my door. "What are you grinning at?" he asked, head canted.

"It's just that your home is kind of perfect, is all."

He bowed gallantly. "You want the grand tour?"

I rested my hand on his outstretched palm and nodded. There was a sizable deck that constructed the porch, complete with two chairs and a small table to enjoy warm evenings. Inside, his furniture in the living area was simple, functional, but everything worked well together to invite a homey feel. The kitchen was large with modern appliances, and the two bedrooms in the back were spacious. One, he had made into an office, and the other was his room. I blushed when I saw his bed. The bedding was nice, dark, and haphazardly thrown in some semblance of order. It was definitely a bed I could find myself comfortable in.

"You hungry?" he asked, deliciously close to my ear.

"Starving, actually."

"I'm not much of a cook, but surely we can put something together from a stocked pantry."

And stocked, it was. Caleb had everything I could possibly imagine in the way of food. I pulled out shelf after rolling shelf of non-perishables and found the refrigerator full as well. "I thought a bachelor would just have frozen pizzas to eat," I murmured in awe.

Caleb yanked the stainless steel freezer door open and stood back. "I have those too if you have a hankerin'."

I laughed at the row of meat lover's specials. "Tempting, but would you mind if I cooked instead?"

A tender expression crossed his face. "You want to cook in here?"

I looked around. "Never cooked in such a fancy kitchen outside of Opal's before."

Slowly, deliberately, he crossed to stand in front of me. His skin smelled masculine and alluring with a faint undertone of animal. He took a breath before he spoke in a tone so velvety soft, it sent a warm sensation to parts of me I hadn't given much thought to before he came into my life.

"Say it. Tell me you need me as much as I need you."

My eyes focused somewhere in the region of his collar bones. If I looked into the brilliant blue of his eyes, I would melt into a useless puddle on the wooden floorboards beneath my feet. "I can't say it now. I need you for safety, and you will always wonder if I said it for the right reasons. It won't count."

"Look at me." He waited until my reluctant gaze met his. "The fact that you just said that will make it count. Say it."

It would be the biggest admission of my life, but he was worth taking the risk. "I need you. And not just for the material stuff. Fixing up my house and trying to get me a job... That stuff doesn't matter. I've needed you from the moment I brought you up to my house. After I killed the grizzly? You had to live, and not just because it would be a weight on my conscience, but because you were the most beautiful thing I ever had in my life, and I couldn't lose you. I knew you wouldn't ever think about me again after you left, but you had to exist."

The tenderness in Caleb's eyes was overwhelming. He leaned forward, placing his hands on the counter behind me. He rested his forehead on mine for just a moment before he kissed me. His lips were as soft as the first time he kissed me on the balcony of the pie shop. I clenched the front of his shirt with my fists, and he stretched forward, parted my lips, demanding more. His hands found my hips, and with ease, he lifted me to sit on the counter. His obvious arousal made me feel powerful. How did I have such an effect on a creature so compelling? His arms snaked around my back and pulled me closer to his body, and I wrapped my legs around him in desperation to be even closer.

"Can I see?" I asked in a ragged breath.

Caleb stopped kissing me, and for a second I thought he would refuse. He eased back slightly and pulled at the top button of his shirt.

I moved my fingertips under his. "Let me."

I pulled at each button in turn and revealed more and more of the still angry red scars. When he shrugged his opened shirt off his broad shoulders, I raked my eyes over every inch of his muscular chest. "You're so—" Words failed me. None were grand enough.

He ran his hand through his hair as if uncomfortable. "Ruined?"

"No. Perfect. You're perfect to me."

His smile was slow, and he ran a light fingertip over the scars on my neck that peeked out from beneath my loose collar. "So are you."

The moment was interrupted with the shrill trumpet of the telephone. Caleb reached across me, apparently not inclined to put any distance between us, and answered it.

There was a muffled murmur of a girl's voice on the other end of the line.

"No, I think I got it," Caleb said, brushing a strand of hair out of my face and tucking it behind my ear. "Hey, Mira says hi."

Dead silence filled the other end. The voice picked up in an excited volume that I could almost understand. He chuckled and handed the phone to me.

Sadey didn't bother with a greeting. "Are you back with Caleb? Tell me you're back together!"

"Yes, we're back together."

His eyes danced, and he inhaled slowly, as if he were savoring a weight being lifted from his shoulders.

A string of incomprehensible shrieks followed, and I handed the phone back to Caleb, then rubbed my throbbing ear.

"Gotta go, Sadey. We'll see you at Sunday dinner." He hung up while Sadey was still mid-question.

The mention of Sunday dinner would have been intimidating if a more desperate fear didn't loom in the forefront. Every minute or so, I thought of the very real danger I was in. Of the danger I put Caleb in by being with him, and it sent a cold bolt of fresh dread skittering up my spine.

He watched my transformation with concern knitted into his blond brows. "What's wrong?"

"I'm scared. Angus won't stop until he finds me."

Caleb watched the waning light out the window as if it held the answers. "Look, he won't find you here. Tomorrow we'll go to the sheriff—"

"But he hates me."

"Hear me out. If he and his deputy ignore us, at least we tried there first. We'll go into the city and find someone who will help. We'll keep at it until somebody takes us seriously and grants you a restraining order against him."

The plan sounded solid enough, and a wave of relief washed over me. I knew he would figure out a way to keep me safe. He was calm in the face of adversity, confident under strenuous situations. It's what made him so good at his job. His self-assurance eased my cowardly bits.

I put my mind to more favorable ventures than dwelling on imminent danger. "I want pasta."

He grinned. "I have a craving for spaghetti myself."

I hopped off the counter and rummaged through the pantry until I found the ingredients I needed. Caleb pulled his shirt on, to my dismay, but left it unbuttoned as a consolation. Eventually, a fire crackled in the fireplace and the smells of a hot meal wafted through his cozy home. I was standing at the stove when he pressed his body behind me.

His hands fell to my hips, and he kissed my neck softly. "Do you need me to do anything?"

"Keep doing that," I said, stifling a moan.

His breath was delectably warm on my neck, and the vibration of his chest rumbled against my back as he chuckled. "Anything else?"

I sighed happily. "Taste this."

Caleb did as instructed and said the spaghetti sauce simmering away in one of his pots was perfect as is.

"Okay, take the garlic bread out of the oven then. Dinner is ready." I gave the Caesar salad one more toss and set it on the small dining table.

We took our time eating. There was no hurry, and our conversation was easy, like before I'd tried to set him free. He asked about my mother, before she'd met Angus, and I shared the good memories I had. Playground visits when I was younger, slip-n-slide summers, and infinite wishes she'd made on dandelions.

"She used to be fun," I explained. "She didn't like raising me by herself, but she always took me to the library and read me books before she tucked me in at night. And on Friday nights, she'd always order us a pizza and rent a cartoon for me from the movie store. I thought we were happy the way things were, but then she met Angus, and she changed. For the better, at first. She practically glowed when he helped around the house and took care of me when her friends asked her to go out for girls' nights. It didn't last, though. He was pretending. That was part of his manipulation, to show her his best side so she'd cling to the way he used to be when he would drink. I always knew he was bad, though. He didn't trick me at all. I didn't care about him, so I could see how hard his eyes looked when he told my mom he loved her. I could see him holding his hands out like he wanted to choke her when her back was turned. They weren't even fighting. He would just do it in passing."

Caleb drew my legs into his lap under the table and leaned back. "He sounds like a piece of work."

I narrowed my eyes playfully. He'd been trying not to curse in front of me since he'd kissed me on the balcony. It was sweet, but I still wanted all of him, the good and the gritty. "You mean piece of shit, don't you?"

"I do. Who took care of you after your mom's funeral? After the trial?"

"No one. No one stepped forward, and I was awarded to the state. Mom didn't have a will to assign a guardian, so I went into a foster home, and they decided something was wrong with me. I went into the hospital soon after that. Stayed there a year, and it was awful, but I was out of control of my memories and feelings. I'd shut down and wasn't doing well with the therapy. I was scared and confused, and every time it came up that I could be released, my doctors denied it. Said I wasn't ready. And maybe I wasn't. I don't know."

"Do you still feel confused about what happened that night?"

He wasn't asking because he didn't believe me. The earnest, worried set to his eyes said he asked because he worried about me keeping everything in. "No. It all cleared up for me. I just needed time. I know what I saw. That memory never wavered. It was just all of the other stuff that became too much."

He massaged the arches of my feet, and I leaned back into the dining chair.

"Do you wish things had been different?" he asked.

"Yeah. Of course I do. I fell through the cracks when my mom died. But then, I guess I'd be living in the city and Uncle Brady never would've taken me in. And I never would've met you." My anger waivered, shifted. I'd been so deeply bitter about what Angus had done, it had tainted me. Jaded me.

But out of the muck, I got Caleb.

A distant smile tugged his lips. "My mom used to take us to this swimming hole in the summers when we were out of school. We'd spend the whole day there. She never got in the water. Said she didn't trust water she couldn't see to the bottom of. I think she was scared of the catfish we would catch out of the tank with my dad. Anyway, I remember she used to collect bathing suits, and I never figured out why. She'd wear a different one every time we went to the tank, but none of them ever got wet as far as I could tell. And all colors, too. She liked bright colors, like Sadey does. It matched her personality. She was happy."

"I wish I could've met her."

"You would've liked her. My dad was really different when she was alive. He wasn't so…hard."

I tried to imagine living without Caleb and decided I'd be really closed off, too, if I sustained that kind of damage to my heart.

I was in awe of Caleb's ease in his own space. It settled something in me, as well. The fire crackled as we cleaned the dishes and put away the leftovers. His hungry eyes fell on me as I emerged from the restroom, newly showered and wearing one of his old T-shirts that draped down to my knees.

I held up my flour dusted clothes. "You mind if I wash these?"

Caleb jerked his head toward the room off the kitchen. "Let me show you how to use the washer and dryer."

I was grateful for his patient teachings. I hadn't ever used a washer before. Uncle Brady had been more of a use-the-sink-and-line-dry type of guy.

While we waited for my clothes to finish their cycle, he turned on a movie, of which I couldn't remember a single scene because Caleb-the-Adonis-McCreedy ran a light touch over the tops of my thighs, draped lazily over his lap for the entirety of the show. He had worked me up to quite the inferno by the end credits.

His attention left the show as I parted my knees and grinned at him. His eyes went round and serious as he ran his hand up the inside of my leg.

"You said you wanted to wait to make our first time special," I said.

"I did." He hooked his finger on the lacy material and pulled my panties down my legs until they reached my ankles. Then, he slowly removed them like he had all the time in the world. I lifted up and pushed his shirt from his shoulders, exposing the long, curving scars on his chest and neck.

"I like the way you look."

"Even marked up like this?"

I couldn't take my eyes from him if I tried. "Especially marked up like this. They are a reminder of what you went through. What we went through the day we really met. These marks are part of our story."

His abdomen flexed with every breath as he stared down at his torso with a frown. "I hadn't thought of them like that."

"How do you see them?"

"They always remind me of what I am now. They don't let me forget the animal Eli put in me."

"Caleb, I love you. And I love your animal, too. That part of you doesn't bother me at all."

"I watch you," he said in a rushed voice. "When I change, I go to your house, and if you're outside working, I watch you from the shadows. When I'm an animal, all I can think about is protecting you and being near you."

"Of hunting for me?"

"Yeah, that too. You aren't mad?"

"I felt you watching me. It scared me at first, but when I knew you were really a bear shifter, I wasn't so scared anymore. I knew you wouldn't ever hurt me." I closed my eyes briefly as he lifted my oversized T-shirt over my head. My nipples puckered as he palmed the weight of my breasts in his hand. God, the man knew how to touch me. Leaning forward, he drew my nipple into his mouth and lapped at it until a warm, tingling sensation zinged rhythmically down my stomach and toward the apex between my legs. I spread my legs wider as he ran his hand down my side and gripped my hip. Slowly, he moved to my other nipple and worked it with his tongue until it was an impossibly tight bud. Sensation flooded me as he unbuttoned the clasp on his jeans and unsheathed his erection. His shaft stood long and thick as he pressed his pants down. I pulled my bottom lip between my teeth in anticipation.

In a graceful movement, he folded me into his arms and carried me into his bedroom. There, he set me gently on his bed and tugged my ankles until my backside reached the edge. Without a word, he lowered himself between my legs and kissed my sex. I gasped.

I should feel shame or discomfort, anything. But right now, all I felt was the tingling sensation Caleb was causing by sucking on my sensitive spot. His tongue plunged into me, and I gripped his hair as my body threatened to shatter to pieces. My legs rested over his shoulders, and my toes curled with every lap of his tongue.

Just as I neared the edge, he eased back. The sound of a foil wrapper filled the room. Could I actually have an orgasm after he stopped touching me? Because right now, it was close.

"Caleb?" I breathed.

"I'm right here, baby," he said, lowering his weight on top of me.

I parted my legs farther to allow him into the cradle of my hips.

The tip of his erection pressed into me in a slow, shallow thrust, and I arched against him. "Please. I'm ready."

His lips found the tripping pulse at my throat and he thrust into me again, a little deeper this time. He was trying to be gentle for my first time, but I felt an acute desperation for more. Rolling my hips against him, I let out the moan that had filled my throat. He pressed in farther, filling and stretching me. It hurt, but he'd done well to prepare me and make sure I was ready for him. The pleasure outweighed the discomfort, and I rocked with him again.

As his arms flexed, I ran my hands up the strong curve of them. He seemed to be holding back so I said, "Look at me."

Another shallow thrust, and he gritted his teeth, easing back. His eyes were the most alluring color. Golds and greens, fire and woods, and as he settled his gaze on me, he looked utterly helpless for a moment. "I can't stop."

Why would I want him too? "Good. Then don't."

With a feral growl, he pressed into me until I could feel his hips against mine. I cried out at how good it felt when he pressed onto the sensitive nub nestled in my slick folds. Tangling his hands with mine, his gaze never left me as he eased into me again, filling me until my insides pulled tight. As I moved with him, he closed his eyes for a moment, and his lips fell to mine. His mouth moved against me, and I opened to allow his tongue to brush mine in a delicious mimic of the penetration that had me straining for release.

The muscles in his arms shook as he gritted his teeth. He turned away for a moment before returning his gaze to mine—a glimpse of the raw lust that he was trying so hard to control. Someday, we'd buck and crash into each other and scream. That much was promised in the barely controlled power Caleb held in check now, but for tonight, he was determined to make this first time comfortable for me. He wouldn't risk hurting me when I was so new and raw. With the realization, I loved him even more.

His hips moved faster and faster until the pressure inside of me became too much. He froze just as I came, and his shaft swelled inside of me and began to pulse in rhythm to my own orgasm.

"Jesus, woman," he rasped against my neck. His teeth grazed the tender skin there, and I held him tighter. "My animal...I feel different."

"Good different or bad different?"

He pulled back, panting. The color of his eyes still blazed unnaturally, but a small smile crooked his sensual lips. "You feel like you're mine now, Mira."

I couldn't help the grin that took my face. That was the best combination of words I'd ever heard. "I was always yours."

"Yeah, but this feels..." His eyes had taken on a faraway look. "It feels really important. Like we're linked or something now. You're my woman."

"No, Caleb. I'm your mate." The word felt right. I was more than his woman or his girlfriend. Something life-altering and permanent had been happening to us since the day I found him bleeding on my land. Tonight had sealed whatever fate we'd fallen into. No more trying to set the other free, or trying to stay away from each other. From here on, it wasn't an option to be apart. Everything in me knew it was true. Caleb disliked what he'd become. He regretted the bear, but that animal side of him had given us something no normal couple could have.

He'd just bonded us.

Chapter Twenty-Two
Caleb

I awoke in the dark. Surprising, because I was an early riser, just not this early. Motionless, I waited for the subtle something that had peeled away the layers of my slumber to reveal itself. Mira lay with her head on my chest, and I stroked her hair to remind myself that she was real. That she was mine.

Silence.

I relaxed, and she stretched her legs with a faint sleep noise. I bent down to kiss her forehead but stopped when light passed over the bedroom window. I lay frozen, hoping my inner bear's gnawing instinct to wake her and flee was wrong somehow. And then I smelled it.

"Mira," I whispered. "Mira, wake up." I shook her gently but urgently.

She tensed and sat ramrod straight. "I smell gasoline."

It wasn't just my imagination then.

"He's here," she said, fear dripping from her strangled whisper. She jolted up and searched in vain for her clothes in the dark. They still sat in a wet puddle in the washer. The best she could do was my pull on my oversized shirt she had worn earlier. "Where are your guns?"

I pulled on my pants and shook my head. "In a gun safe at my dad's house."

"You don't have any weapons here." She hadn't asked but stated it with a twinge of defeat in her voice.

I yanked the phone off the receiver and pushed the talk button with more force than necessary. No dial tone. "Phone's not working."

"He cut the phone lines. You have a cell phone?"

I checked my cell for the hundredth time since I'd moved in with the same results. "Zero reception out here. I have to drive up the road by your place to get any bars."

She cursed quietly as I led her into the kitchen. I pulled the biggest knife I owned out of the butcher's block and secured it into the back of my jeans. The metal was cold and unforgiving against my skin, but I didn't mind. It reminded me that it was there.

"McCreedy, send my girl on out here," a man drawled. The voice of Angus French was as cold as the blade behind me. "My beef ain't with you."

Dull moonlight threw lines across her face through the blinds, and I could see that Mira's eyes had gone black like they used to. She was listening to the voice of her nightmares, and I wanted to kill him for scaring her like this.

"I won't let him hurt you."

"McCreedy!" Angus screamed.

"What do you want?" I yelled through the door. I opened the blinds and saw the silhouette of the man. His face was completely dark with the moon behind him, and he leaned heavily against an old, black sedan. Inside, a large dog barked relentlessly.

"What do you mean, what do I want? I want to lay eyes on my little girl I haven't seen in all these years. I want to see if she's still as pretty as I remember. Toss her out here, and you won't get hurt."

"Ain't gonna happen, Angus."

"Well," he drawled slowly. "That's what I 'spected you'd say, so I'm going to lay down a couple of ground rules. Don't go trying to sneak out the back door 'cause I have it good and rigged. I'll hear any attempt and throw this cigarette I've been draggin' on at your house. I've doused it pretty good in lighter fluid so I 'spect it'll go up pretty quick. Awful way to die, so I hear."

I leaned my head against the window pane and ran through ten escape plans in a second. None would work. Mira's nails dug into the palm of my hand.

"Why are you doing this?" I asked him.

"Because that little bitch—" Angus cleared his throat and chuckled, a chilling sound. "Because my little girl and I have some unfinished business. Business that don't involve you, McCreedy. Now hurry this up. I ain't known for my patience, boy."

"Caleb," Mira said. "Can you change into your animal?"

Regret made me swallow hard. "I don't control the changes. They always come at night, but I haven't figured out a reason or a trigger for them."

"It's okay. I don't want you getting hurt. I'll be okay."

"No. You aren't going out there with that lunatic."

"We'll both burn alive in here. You heard him. He doesn't bluff."

"Stay here." I pushed her gently back and opened the door before she could protest. "I'm coming out to talk." I held my hands up in surrender.

I didn't make it farther than the doorway before Angus flung a rifle up faster than I thought possible and pulled the trigger. A yelp of surprised pain burst from me as fire seared through my leg. I couldn't hold weight on it anymore and fell forward like a stone.

"Caleb!" Mira shrieked.

Angus got to me before she could. "Sorry, boy," he said through stale breath and cigarette smoke. "I thought you were shorter. I was going for a gut shot. This one'll be a little slower." The apologies of a serial killer.

Mira had disappeared from the doorway for a second but returned with a knife raised high over her head. Her face said she meant it when she aimed the tip at Angus French's face. He caught her hand and wrenched it until she cried out and dropped the blade. I took the distraction to pull my own knife, and with all of the force I could muster from my disadvantaged position, I thrust it into his leg and pulled down with one swift motion. "Run, Mira!"

Angus fell backward with a roar of pain. In a flash of anger, he swung his rifle like a baseball bat directly down onto my head.

Everything went black.

****

Mira

"No, no, no," I chanted as grief washed over me. It mingled with my fear and created a cloud of horror, then somber acceptance. The sound of the butt of the gun as it connected with Caleb's head was a noise that would haunt me for the last few minutes of my life. I knelt down and fluttered my fingers helplessly over his fallen body. The upper leg of his jeans looked black in the dim light from the blood that seeped out of him. Angus scuffled as he righted himself behind me, and the glint of the knife I had dropped gleamed from just out of my reach. Scrambling backward, I tried to kick the door closed before he could catch me, but Angus was fast. If anything, prison had only made him stronger.

He caught my hair and yanked it backward, bringing water to my eyes. He didn't wait for me to stand to ease the pressure. Angus simply dragged me out of the house by the roots. From the puddle of crimson-colored liquid beside Caleb, my flailing legs made red arcs and circles across the wooden floorboards with my struggles.

Angus hoisted me up and put my face against the window of the black sedan. The dog inside was massive. Thickly muscled and gnashing his huge teeth at the window in desperation to get at me. A trained killer, just like Angus.

"You know what I missed the most while I was in prison, sugar? Coon hunts. There is nothing quite like the thrill of the chase when you are hunting down a big ol' coon."

I closed my eyes tightly against the vision of the dog mere millimeters away from my face and blocked out the barking. I had to get away. I had to get help for Caleb.

"I'll give you five minutes head start." Angus eased back and looked me in the eye. His wrinkles were deeper, but his black, bottomless eyes still held the same icy emptiness I remembered. The man had been born wicked. He'd apparently accepted that a long time ago, embraced it even. Now, there was no soul left in him at all. "I think that's pretty generous, don't you? Five minutes, and I let old Brutus here loose. He's a bully, for sure, but he's a good tracker, too. A Brutus of all trades." Angus chuckled at his joke, and I held my breath against the stale rot that emanated from his mouth. "When he catches you, and he will, I'll be right behind him to put you out of your misery. What was it your boyfriend said? Oh, yeah." His grip in my hair loosened. "Run, Mira."

Angus shoved me forward, and I hesitated just a second to determine if he was going to shoot me in the back. It wasn't his style. Too fast. Too painless. I ran straight for the north side of Caleb's property. I ran for my haunted woods.

One mile, give or take. That was the distance between where my feet beat furiously at the ground and my house, full of all my favorite weapons. I was no match for the dog, true. But these were my woods. I knew them like the back of my hand, and using them was my best shot at getting help for Caleb.

I ran for my life. Low-lying limbs struck my face and arms, stinging my skin. They only made me run faster. I lost track of time, but Brutus would be coming for me soon. My knees buckled as I skidded to a stop. A quick glance around and I circled the area in panic. For lack of anything else, I wrenched a handful of my hair out and threw it across a bush before I grabbed a tree branch and swung myself over a pile of brambles. No sooner did my feet hit the ground then I was sprinting again. It wouldn't slow Brutus down for long, but even seconds could make a difference.

I viciously ripped a small branch off a tree and kept running.

Stabbing it into the palm of my hand, I clenched my teeth against the pain, then smeared the trickling blood onto trees and brush farther off my trail. I tossed the bloodied branch in the opposite direction just as the demon dog bayed. He'd caught my scent somewhere down the hill.

A gasp escaped my lips as I ruthlessly shoved dirt into the wound to stop the bleeding. He was coming, and when I glanced behind me, I could see his dark body moving with violent intent toward me. Just when I thought he would catch me, a flurry of movement burst from the thicket. I watched the snarling ball of gnashing teeth for a moment before I realized what was happening. Brady, my loyal, mangy mutt was risking his life to give me time. I grabbed a stick to help him but a shot fired and ricocheted off a rock beside me. Angus was too close, and I hadn't a chance at pulling the dogs apart. I wouldn't waste the time Brady was trying to give me.

I ran.

I bolted for the old tool shed. From the sounds of Brutus's howls, the house was too far away to make it before he was on me. I flung the storage door open and squinted through the dusty dark. My hands searched frantically and fell onto the cold metal of the weapon that would have to do.

Brutus was so close. Angus's taunts reached out for me like black, snaking tendrils.

There was a short wooden fence that backed to the shed and an old overturned wagon on the other side, which effectively created a bottleneck. I would be trapped, and if my plan didn't work, I'd die and so would Caleb. Couldn't think like that right now, though. It just had to work.

Prying the ancient metal trap open wasn't easy. My hands were sweating and bloody, and I had to use my foot as leverage to keep it open while I put the pin in. A vision of it clamping down on me was my only company. I kicked dry leaves over the trap and reopened my hand with a loose nail that jutted out from the fence. A long line of red dripped over the trap as long as I dared before I cowered as far against the fence as I could, clutching my throbbing hand to my chest.

Brutus's eyes shined eerily, and he growled, deep in his throat. The game had come to an end. He would get his reward, and he slowed like he was savoring his victory. Stepping into the entrance of my trap, he stopped, perhaps sensing the danger. He paced and sniffed the ground suspiciously. A wave of panic overcame me that my plan would fail, and I looked frantically for a way to escape my self-made prison. Brutus sniffed the air, likely encouraged with the scent of my fear, and stepped forward, nose down. I jumped as the trap closed loudly around the dog's legs. He bayed a yelp that echoed through my woods.

I covered my mouth with my hand and allowed a sob as I edged around the snarling, snapping animal, still intent on my demise over the pain it was in. The house was in sight, and my screaming muscles protested moving again. My body shook from shock. My feet were bloody and swollen but Angus was so close, I could hear him.

"I didn't get a chance to see the necklace I made for you all healed up," he said, emerging from a thicket. "I bet it looks nice on you, Mira."

I wanted to wretch at such a soulless compliment. Caleb was running out of time and adrenaline was still feeding my blood with desperation to save him, so I bolted for the barn. The house was too far but the barn was a maybe. I flung myself over the fence and limped to the shelter. The horses ran, white shades in the dark, and I whimpered with the realization that I was backed into the corner of the barn and out of weapons. I turned in a desperate circle, searching for anything I could use against him.

"Hoo, hoo," Angus sang softly as he leaned his rifle against the barn. "What a pretty little barn owl I've found. You killed my dog, you naughty little owl."

"You killed my dog, too," I shot back.

Angus paused and then chuckled. "Still crazy then, Mira? I never saw no dog. I was shooting at you. Missed on purpose, though. It's more fun this way."

I reared back to hit him, but he grabbed my fist with an iron grip. My bones felt as if they were ground to dust, and I screamed at the blistering pain. Tears ran down the sides of my face as I clutched my ruined hand against my stomach.

Angus wrapped slow hands around my throat and pressed me against the barn wall. "Your mother was a disappointment. Shooting her? I should have planned it differently. There is something…" Angus looked up at the sky, as if searching for the right word. "Sweeter, when you feel the life drain out of someone. A bullet robbed me of that high. I won't be disappointed with you, though." He leaned close to my ear and whispered, "You've done so well."

My legs flailed as he tightened his grip and lifted me off my feet. The wall behind me splintered but held. His bottomless, black eyes sparked with excitement when I kicked my feet. I made small croaking sounds as the corners of my vision blurred, and just as I thought it would be easier to give up, a figure lumbered toward us in the moonlight.

Uncle Brady, back from the dead, stumbled slowly toward Angus's back. He was a blood-covered zombie, and I tried desperately to hold on to consciousness. Not Uncle Brady, I realized as the figure drew closer. Caleb.

He threw his head back, and an enormous grizzly bear exploded from him. I fought desperately to stay conscious. The bear padded closer, bigger than I thought possible. His muscles flexed and twitched with every graceful step, and though he walked with a deep limp, it didn't seem to hinder him. His lips pulled back from impossibly long, sharp teeth as his muscles gathered under him.

He was too late.

I was slipping away and couldn't hold on any longer. Angus frowned at my attention and looked behind him, just in time to see the twelve foot grizzly charge. We both fell hard. I crawled on my hands and knees, gasping for my life as a flurry of violent motion took up most of the space in the barn. Caleb sank his teeth into Angus's throat and held on through my stepfather's struggles. And eventually, Angus didn't move anymore. Caleb had made sure he wouldn't be turned and gifted with the power of an animal. He made sure he was dead—that he would never hurt me again.

My throat felt swollen shut, and I couldn't drag enough air into my lungs to give relief.

I was panicking, scratching at my neck when Caleb changed back to his human form with a series of pops and a grunt of pain.

"How?" I croaked out as he reached me.

"I drove your truck over here. Breathe, Mira. Shh. Just relax and breathe. It's all over. I called the police from down the road. They'll be here any minute."

Chapter Twenty-Three
Mira

Caleb passed out before help arrived. He looked pale, and his flesh was cold to the touch. I watched the precarious rise and fall of his chest like it was my salvation as I put all my weight onto the seeping wound on his leg with the cleanest saddle blanket I had found. The only things keeping him alive now were his bear and me.

When they loaded him into the ambulance, Sheriff Clancy tried to strong-arm me out of the way.

"No!" I screamed, sobs wracking my body. "I'm going with him." I let my anguish show as I pleaded with the paramedics. "Please. He's mine."

"We don't have time for this," a stout lady who worked furiously over Caleb's body said. "She needs to go to the clinic, anyway. Let her in."

I hopped up behind the paramedics and gave Sheriff Clancy the finger. It hurt like hell on injured hands but the scowl on his face made it worth it.

"I'm coming by for your official statement tonight, Fletcher. No leaving town," he yelled as we sped away.

A second ambulance passed us on the way out, probably to pick up Angus. They didn't have a shot in hell at saving him. I'd seen what Caleb's bear had done to his throat.

A helicopter landed in a vacant lot behind the clinic, and Caleb was care lifted to a big hospital in the city. The nurse said the clinic wasn't equipped for that kind of head trauma. I, however, was a perfect candidate for clinic medicine. Ruined hands and feet, twisted ankles, and lacerations over my face and arms. A swollen and bruised neck where perfect fingerprints could be seen. The deputy, Young, took pictures of my injuries before they cleaned me up. His brown eyes were sad and sympathetic, and he told me the pictures would help to build a case against the monster who did this to me.

Numbness fell over me like a blanket. Without Caleb here to save, my reserves were spent. I didn't talk, but my silence wasn't the confused or traumatized kind like the first time when Angus had killed my mother. I was simply too tired to make conversation. The nurses tossed around worried glances and talked quietly outside the door before administering a sedative to help me sleep.

Sadey showed up early the next morning just before the clinic discharged me. She somberly held out a bag of clothes and helped me dress.

I was afraid of the answer so I stalled and pulled my hair back before I asked, "Is he okay?"

Sadey shrugged and leaned against the thin clinic mattress, misery written over every tired feature. "He hasn't woken up yet. They don't know if he will. Said it's just a waiting game now."

Bending, she slid flip-flops over my bandaged feet and pushed my wheelchair out to her waiting car. After I was tucked in and had waved the nurse away, Sadey sat in the driver's seat, then grimly gripped the steering wheel. "Angus French is dead." Sadey tilted her head and waited for a reaction from me that wouldn't come.

I didn't know how to feel. Sorrow at the deepest betrayal from someone who was supposed to protect me? Anger with him, with the system that released him, with my fate? Relief over the death of someone I knew but hated?

I stared blankly ahead and watched a mother tote two small children into the clinic. "Thanks for telling me."

"Mira? Are you okay?" Sadey's eyelashes were wet with unshed tears.

I tried to smile reassuringly but was pretty sure I failed. "If Caleb is okay, then I will be, too." It was the best I could offer her.

Sadey wiped her eyes with her fingertips and pulled out of the parking lot. "I talked to Opal this morning. She's coming to visit you today at the big hospital while we wait for Caleb to wake up. Said she's bringing you a slice of devil's food cake in honor of your stepdaddy."

I snorted and covered my mouth with my gauzed hand. I wanted to laugh and cry and scream all at once.

The waiting room of the hospital was filled with a thick, quiet somberness. Some people I recognized. Caleb's family, one of the men who worked on the rig with him, Becca. The others I didn't know. The man I cared for was beloved by a town that respected his family. A momentary panic hit me when I entered the room and all of those eyes slid to me. Did they blame me for their fallen hero? What did they think as I stood in front of them, bandaged and bruised, unable to hold any of their gazes?

"Over here," Caleb's father said, waving his hand slightly to be seen over another row of seats.

I smiled at Sadey. "It's okay. You go sit with your family. I'll go to the cafeteria or something."

Sadey's eyebrows, just a shade darker than her blond hair, drew down. "He's talking to you."

I glanced at Mr. McCreedy in question, and he gestured again. Sadey and I picked our way around people sitting on the floor, and he offered me his seat.

"It's all right. I'll just sit on the floor if that's okay." I gestured with my bandaged hand to the comfortable expanse of purple and yellow printed carpet.

Evan pulled his head out of his hands. "Mira, you look like shit. Sit down before you make everyone in here uncomfortable." He stood and pressed my shoulder until I sat in his chair, then he took a seat on the carpet near me.

The chairs were wide enough for two slim girls to fit in. "Sit by me?" I asked Sadey.

When we were settled, Mr. McCreedy cleared his throat quietly. "I was mistaken about how much you meant to my son, Mira. He brought you to me for my approval, and I kept it from him. From you."

I stopped him, unable to stomach more. "Sir, you don't have to apologize to me. You were trying to protect him in your own way. You're a good father."

Mr. McCreedy's breath hitched, and he rubbed a shaking hand through his graying hair. Sadey rushed to him and sat in his lap. "He'll be okay, Dad. He's tough."

In a move that shocked me into momentary stillness, Mr. McCreedy wrapped Sadey and me into a hug.

I fluttered my hand lightly onto his back and searched for something to ease his worry. "You raised a strong boy, Mr. McCreedy. Caleb is very brave. He went through hell to save me. He'll come back to us." I hoped with an overwhelming desperation that the last part was true.

Mr. McCreedy released us, then rubbed his hand over the stubble on his face and sniffed. "You guys hungry?"

Sadey and I shook our heads, though by all rights, I should've been. I hadn't eaten since the spaghetti dinner at Caleb's house last night.

"I'm starved," Evan volunteered.

"Brian? Emily?" Mr. McCreedy asked. "Let's go to the cafeteria and grab some lunch. I need a breather."

A dark-headed woman, Emily, Caleb's other sister, waved to me and introduced herself on the way out. She didn't even treat me like a leper. Mr. McCreedy gave Joseph Reyes strict instructions to come find us the millisecond a doctor came with news. Outside of the waiting room, I inhaled deeply. It was much easier to breathe without half the town's watchful eyes on me.

A half a chicken sandwich, a cup of green Jell-O cubes, and a handful of pain pills later, and I felt much better physically. That could have been partly due to the pain meds. The next time I decided to go gallivanting through a mile of rough woods in the dead of night, I'd have to remind myself that normal people wore shoes.

As we sat in the booth, full of hospital food and all exhausted from a long night, I took in the soft murmur of the McCreedy family. It was comfortable to be among them when Evan's insults weren't directed at me. Sadey braided my tangled hair and chimed in on the conversation about how they'd have to take shifts at the hospital when Evan and Mr. McCreedy would have to go back to work tomorrow. Was this what it was like to be part of a family? This feeling of belonging?

My head snapped up when Joseph Reyes came jogging through the cafeteria, scanning the tables. "Joseph," I hailed him.

"He's awake," he said excitedly before he even reached us. "They're allowing family only, but he asked for Mira to come in there, too."

"Oh, my God," I murmured as the tears I'd been holding back spilled down my cheeks. He was alive, and now awake, and it dawned on me that we'd survived together. Overwhelmed, I squeezed back when Sadey grabbed my hand. A sob wrenched from me as the metal of my chair screeched against the tile floor. I followed Mr. McCreedy at a run down the hallway and up a flight of stairs. The others trailed just behind us.

"You go on," Caleb's dad offered when we reached the door. "He wants to see you first. We'll talk to his doctor and be in there in a few minutes."

"Okay," I whispered through trembling lips. Hurriedly, I wicked the moisture from my cheeks and took a long, steadying breath, then pushed open the door.

Monitors beeped, and the room was cold and generic, drowning in clean white. Caleb lay on the bed, quiet and still as death. The small bandage on his head didn't seem to do his injury justice, and the thin sheets lumped over his misshapen leg. *He must have a cast.* His closed eyes threatened to buckle my knees. I hadn't realized how badly I wanted to see the vivid blue in his eyes until right now. I had to focus on the positives. The color in his cheeks was back, and he was cleaned up. His leg seemed to rest comfortably enough under the sheets, and his face was relaxed, as if he didn't feel any pain.

And he was alive.

It could've been so much worse. I reached for his hand and smiled at the familiarity of his warm palm against mine.

"Hey," Caleb said in a hoarse whisper. "Come here."

I swallowed hard, fighting back tears of relief at the crooked smile I so loved on him. "Will I hurt you?"

"Nah. I don't think I'd feel anything right now," he said with a chuckle.

The bed creaked under my added weight, and he reached up to touch the side of my face. "Remember that time you saved me from Eli?"

I nodded, unable to speak through the thick emotion that churned ceaselessly inside me.

"Now I saved you back."

I huffed a laugh and wiped my eyes. I kissed his hand for a long time, trying to control my ragged emotions. He'd used these hands to bring me back to life. To fix my house and to hold me. To protect me. My vision blurred and warmth trickled down my cheeks as I dragged my gaze to his.

Because of him, I'd never have to hide again.

"You saved me in more ways than you know."

Epilogue
Mira

A plastic bag, half-full of pecans, crinkled as the wind whipped around me. I scoured the earth for another and marveled at everything my woods had taken and given me in return. My fingertips flicked away dry leaves of autumn and fell on a solid weight to fill my palm. I jerked my gaze at a rustle of movement and searched for my old, mangy dog. Half of the town had helped me scour my woods for him years ago, but there was no evidence he had ever existed. I still imagined him running wild out in the forest somewhere, happy. I'd probably always look for him.

Sheriff Clancy still didn't like me much and definitely didn't like the way Angus had died with his throat ripped out and no feasible explanation. He was just being stubborn, though, as everyone else in town had accepted me over time. I had friends now, but most importantly, I had a family in the McCreedys. I was one of them now. I stood and rubbed my hand over the swell of my belly and smiled at the answering movement from my little one. Soon, there would be a new McCreedy to add to the family tree.

Soft footsteps told me of Caleb's approach. In a gesture so simple but so profound, he touched the small of my back and took the burden of the bag from my hands. A smile and an easy word brought a shift to my heart that only came when he was near. He touched my growing stomach with such reverence, I thanked my lucky stars for the hundredth time that he'd decided he wanted a family with me.

I was happy here with him because I had known sorrow. Our scars, long healed, told of an iron strength that replaced our fear.

We stood, looking over our woods, connected by intertwined fingers, my bear man and me.

The ghosts had rattled free, and the shadows no longer held menace.

My ghosts had rattled free.

I was free.

Acknowledgements

First off, a big thanks goes to you, readers. I'm a huge fan of yours and because of you, I get to do what I love, which is storytelling. Also to my lovely editor, Corinne DeMaagd, for polishing this story. I've had the great pleasure of working with her before on several projects, and was able to convince her to join Team Werebear. I absolutely adore her work and have read several books she's done, and was thrilled when she agreed to edit for me. For my own alpha male and our two little cubs, for putting up with my deadline week pajama wardrobe and strange hours. And lastly, a huge thanks to the authors I've met through this incredible journey, who are always there and willing to offer advice. These books wouldn't be if I didn't have such an incredible team behind me.

Want more from T. S. Joyce?

Read on for a sneak peek of the first book in the bestselling Bear Valley Shifters series.

The Witness and the Bear

(Bear Valley Series, Book 1)

By T. S. Joyce

THE WITNESS AND THE BEAR
(Bear Valley Shifters, Book 1)

Chapter One

Today was as good a day to die as any.

Jimmy's fingers dug into her shoulder as he shoved her out the window. "Hannah! Stop fighting me. If you don't run now, it'll be too late."

Another tremendous crash rattled the room. Stone's men were coming in sooner than later and the men protecting her were sitting ducks to the hell on the other side of that door. Jeremy watched her with an eerie glow to his dark eyes. Fluorescent lights and dingy walls had that effect on him. Braced against the door, he snarled, "Get out of here!"

"And what about you?" she snapped, lunging for the window and gripping the edges with straining fingers. "Huh? They'll kill you! There is no end to their reach. They'll keep coming until I'm dead and I'm tired of running. Just let them have me."

Defeated. After the last time they'd found her, she'd skimmed the insanity train. Paranoia ruled her life. And not the I-smoked-a-joint-and-now-the-government-is-after-me kind. This fear didn't end with the high. It stretched on and on until she would drown in it. Burn in it. Fall into the darkness wider than the known world and tumble forever, hitting every rock crevice on the way down until her mind was shredded. She was so damned tired of it.

"I'll never forgive you," Jeremy said. His cold eyes threw ice that pierced her heart. Gray hair cropped short, wrinkles that textured his face, and most of them were probably from trying to keep her safe for the past year. Witness protection gone horribly wrong. He'd given too much for her to give up now. He knew it, and begrudgingly, she knew it too.

"Jimmy," she breathed, tears burning her eyes.

His grip on her shirt tightened and he shook his head, slow. Bright blue eyes filled with sadness so deep, she didn't know how he could draw a breath. Jimmy and Jeremy wouldn't come with her this time. Their last stand would be here, in this filthy apartment in Ashland, Oregon.

Crash. Plaster spewed from the walls and ceiling and Jimmy shoved her out onto the fire escape. "Climb down and run. Don't stop until you know they aren't following. Take this." He shoved a Glock into the palm of her hand, the metal cold against the perspiration of fear. "Shoot 'em if you're cornered."

Jeremy flew backward with the force of the next blow and Jimmy shoved her in the back. She fell forward, catching the grate with her knees and crying out at the sudden pain. Gunfire peppered the tiny space and she tumbled down the stairs, caught herself on the railing at the bottom and shot one last look to the window, then pounded the pavement with the soles of her sneakers.

Jeremy who'd given up his life as a civilian to protect her. Jeremy, who'd calmed her fears when Stone's men got too close. Jeremy, who'd become more like father figure than friend. He was trapped in the middle of the rattling explosions.

A sob wrenched from her throat. The last good parts of her would die with him. His death was on her. She'd made the choice to testify against Stone and his men, and that decision had caused an earthquake that rippled through her life and killed people she cared about. If she lived a minute or a decade, she'd never curse another person with her love.

A hand reached out from the darkness and wrapped around her throat like a manacle. She tried to scream but her wind wouldn't come through his crushing grasp and as the man emerged from the shadows, the flickering street light illuminated a long scar across his forehead.

Spinning, he slammed her against a brick wall hard enough to rattle her skull and blur her vision. Sparks whipped this way and that through the edges of her vision and warmth trickled down her neck. Yanking her long, honey colored hair out of the way, the man grunted a satisfied noise and the crack of metal on metal was deafening as he cocked his gun.

Definitely one of Stone's enforcers. No one else would be interested in the scar that marked her.

Gravel met the flesh of her cheek as he slammed her to the ground, and when his weight disappeared, she rolled over. No way was she going to die with a bullet in her back. The least this asshole could do was look in her eyes when he pulled that trigger. Gunfire had tapered off from above, and the apartment behind his shoulder had gone dark. Her breath trembled, filling the night air with the traitorous proof of her fear. Heart hammering against her sternum, she glared at the sneering man.

"Go to hell," he said, lifting the barrel.

"You first," she snarled, pulling the trigger on the Glock Jimmy had gifted her.

His gun discharged at the exact same moment as hers, and pain ripped through her, shredding her insides until there was nothing left. The man sank to his knees with a shocked look as his unloaded weapon clattered to the cracked pavement. She struggled to breathe as he brought searching fingertips to his chest and pulled them back crimson.

The last thing she'd do on this earth was rid it of an evil man. Pride surged through her as he fell forward. Her hand lay limp in front of her, smattered with blood. It felt detached from her body. Everything did. Nothing worked except her lungs, dragging air in, and pushing it out, and even that small movement was failing.

The man's eyes dimmed until the dark orbs saw nothing at all. Her lungs rattled with every breath, but she smiled despite the pain. Stone won the war, but at least she'd go out on this tiny victory.

Her vision shattered inward and she winced at the blinding pain.

Nearby, an animal roared loud enough to rattle her bones.

If it was her death the creature sought, he was too late.

She was already gone.

The Witness and the Bear, as well as the entire Bear Valley Shifters series, are available now. To read more about how Hannah finds love in a clan of legendary bear shifters, find her story on Amazon.

"It'll take an alpha to save her from the man she testified against."

About the Author

T.S. Joyce

T.S. Joyce is devoted to bringing hot shifter romances to readers. Hungry alpha males are her calling card, and the wilder the men, the more she'll make them pour their hearts out. She werebear swears there'll be no swooning heroines in her books. It takes tough-as-nails women to handle her shifters.

    Experienced at handling an alpha male of her own, she lives in a tiny town, outside of a tiny city, and devotes her life to writing big stories. Foodie, wolf whisperer, ninja, thief of tiny bottles of awesome smelling hotel shampoo, nap connoisseur, movie fanatic, and zombie slayer, and most of this bio is true.

Bear Shifters? Check
Smoldering Alpha Hotness? Double Check
Sexy Scenes? Fasten up your girdles, ladies and gents, it's gonna to be a wild ride.

For more information on T. S. Joyce's work, visit her website at www.tsjoycewrites.wordpress.com

Printed in Great Britain
by Amazon